The Ivory City

Marcus Crouch

THE IVORY CITY

and other stories from
INDIA and PAKISTAN

with illustrations by
William Stobbs

PELHAM BOOKS

to the memory of
ARNOLD BAKE
who showed me the real India

Acknowledgements

I am indebted to
Keith Salkeld, Kent County Library
and Peggy Richards for the loan of source material

This edition first published in Great Britain by
Pelham Books Ltd, 44 Bedford Square,
London WC1B 3DU
1980

ISBN 0 7207 1188 6

Filmset and printed by
BAS Printers Limited, Over Wallop, Hampshire
and bound by
Hunter & Foulis Ltd., Edinburgh

Contents

Under the Banyan Tree

It had been a hot day. It always was, at least for nine months and more in every year, in the great plain through which Mother Ganga rolled unhurriedly towards the sea. Everyone in the village from priest to sweeper had given in to the heat by mid-morning, and had found a shady corner in which to doze away the hours when the sun was at its highest.

Now, towards evening, it was, if not cool, a great deal more bearable. Like the Sleeping Beauty's court the village came to life, yawned and stretched itself. Yes, there was no doubt about it. Evening was the best time of all in India. Too late to start working, too early for bed, evening was the time for enjoyment.

It was also, by a custom which went back beyond man's imagining, storytime. There was no organised entertainment, and only rarely did a travelling troupe of singers and dancers stop in such an insignificant village. No, the entertainment was stored in men's heads. There was not a man in the community who did not have his hoard of exciting or sad or funny tales remembered from earliest childhood.

Not that everyone was a performer. The art of telling stories aloud in public was a skilled one, and only a few in any place had mastered it. Here in our steaming village it was a boy who told stories better than anyone. During the day Horidash was just like any other boy, running around the bazaar with nothing but a rag tied around the waist, chased by irritable shopkeepers, not above a little stealing when he was hungry—which was most of the time.

See Horidash now! As the light fades, people drift down to the meeting-place by the big banyan tree where a few small lanterns have been lit. When all are settled and as quiet as Indian crowds will ever be, Horidash appears. He has found—heaven knows where—a strip of gold cloth, and he has wound this around his skinny body. He walks with great dignity to the open space left for him, strikes a pose, and in his high, clear, penetrating voice, he begins:

'In a certain village there lived a poor Brahman who had married a wife . . .'

The Fish Supper

The Brahman's wife awoke one morning with a great appetite. 'Now what I should like for dinner', she said to her husband, 'is a really nice bit of *koi* fish. Just run along to the market and get me some.'

'Very well, my dear,' said the Brahman. So he went along to the market, and there on a stall were some very fine fish. He bought three big ones and took them home. She was mightily pleased, and she cleaned them and put them on the fire, so that the rich smell of cooking went right through the house. How good they were!

At dinner-time, the Brahman said, 'I shall eat two of these fish.'

'Oh no, you won't,' said his wife. 'I'm having two.'

'Nonsense!' said the Brahman. 'I am the master of this house, and a holy man into the bargain. I deserve respect and the biggest helping.'

'Biggest fiddlesticks,' said the wife. 'What do you think I am, the servant?'

'I went and got them.'

'So you did, but they wouldn't be much good without my cooking.'

'Remember who I am, woman,' shouted the Brahman. 'I am your husband and your lord. Besides, I'm hungrier than you are.'

'Don't forget I am your wife. You swore to love and cherish me. And I am a good cook, too, and don't forget it.'

What pigheads they were! Neither of them would give way, and they got angrier and angrier, and hungrier and hungrier. At last the Brahman said: 'Right! Let's go to bed. We shall lie there in silence, and the one who speaks first will get the single fish.'

'Very well.' So there they lay, side by side in silence, while their food got cold. Day faded from the sky and it was night. All through the darkness, neither said a word. Dawn came and morning went by. Still not a word.

The neighbours began to worry. They were usually

a noisy couple, and yet not a sound came from the house. One by one friends knocked on the door and called out, but there was never a reply. It was most puzzling. At last the neighbours decided that something serious must have happened. Perhaps they had been taken ill and died in the night. So they broke down the door and went in. There lay the silly couple, with their eyes wide open, silent. The neighbours lifted them and dropped them again, but still there was never a sound out of either of them.

'Oh dear, oh dear!' said one of their friends. 'They must be dead. We must hold the funeral at once.' So, sadly, and playing solemn music, they carried the silent couple in procession to the river-bank where bodies were burnt. The mourners built a tall bed of logs and laid the Brahman on top. Then, weeping, they took the wife and put her beside her husband. One of them picked up a flaming torch and set the funeral pyre alight.

The flames swept up and licked the Brahman's foot. He jumped up with a yell and shouted: 'I'll eat the one.'

'Then I'll have the two,' screamed his wife in triumph, and she too jumped down from the burning wood.

The neighbours were amazed to see their friends come to life and to hear their cries. They decided at once that the two had become man-eating ghosts and were coming after them. They ran for their lives, with the Brahman and his wife close behind, still shouting, 'I'll eat one,' and 'I'll eat two.'

So at last they got home, where they sat down to eat yesterday's dinner for today's late breakfast. The Brahman made do with one fish, while his wife made a pig of herself with two.

Lambikin

One morning Lambikin set out to call on his Granny.
He danced along on his long thin legs, jumping high in
the air at the thought of all the good things she would
give him to eat.

Very soon he met a jackal, who said: 'Lambikin!
Lambikin! I shall eat you.'

Lambikin just gave a little frisk and said:

> 'Don't be so hasty.
> I'll taste much more tasty
> When I've gobbled Granny's pasty.'

This made good sense to the jackal, and so he let Lambikin go on.

In a little while he came to a vulture in a tree, and the vulture looked down and said: 'Lambikin! Lambikin! I will eat you.'

Lambikin just gave a little frisk and said:

> 'Don't be so hasty.
> I'll taste much more tasty
> When I've gobbled Granny's pasty.'

This made good sense to the vulture, and so he let Lambikin go on.

Now on his journey Lambikin met, one by one, a tiger and a wolf and a dog and an eagle, and each said, as he saw the fine juicy little lamb: 'Lambikin! Lambikin! I shall eat you.'

And to each of them Lambikin replied, giving a little frisk:

> 'Don't be so hasty.
> I'll taste much more tasty
> When I've gobbled Granny's pasty.'

So at last he came to his Granny's house, and he said, all of a hurry: 'Hello, Granny. I've promised to get fat. You have always said that I must keep my word, so just put me in the corn bin, if you please.'

Granny thought that he was being very greedy, but she put him in the corn bin, and he stayed there for seven days, eating and eating and eating until he was so fat that he nearly filled the bin from side to side.

Then his Granny said that he was fat enough for anything and must now go home. 'I can't go home like this,' said Lambikin. 'I look so fat and tasty that some animal is sure to eat me up. This is what you must do,' said the plump little lamb. 'Take the skin of my poor little brother who died, and make it into a little drum. Then I can sit inside and roll along the road quite safely, because I'm tight like a drum myself.'

So this is what Granny did. She made a little drumikin out of the sheepskin, with the wool inside, and Lambikin squeezed inside and curled up, just as snug as could be, then he set the drum rolling.

Soon he met the eagle, who said:

'Drumikin! Drumikin!
Have you seen Lambikin?'

Lambikin, curled up warm and safe, called out:

'Fell in the fire, and so will you.
Rub-a-dum! Rub-a-dum!'

'There goes my dinner,' said the eagle, and Lambikin went rolling along the road, singing 'Rub-a-dum! Rub-a-dum!'

On his way he met all the animals, one by one, and each one asked him:

'Drumikin! Drumikin!
Have you seen Lambikin?'

And to each of them the naughty Lambikin sang:

'Fell in the fire, and so will you.
Rub-a-dum! Rub-a-dum doo!'

And dog and wolf and tiger and vulture all went off hungry, missing their dinner of fat Lambikin.

At last, along came the jackal, all skin and bones and

shabby coat, but cunning as cunning. He called out:

> 'Drumikin! Drumikin!
> Have you seen Lambikin?'

And Lambikin sang, lying warm in his little bed and chirping like a cricket:

> 'Fell in the fire, and so will you.
> Rub-a-dum! Rub . . .'

But the jackal knew his voice in a flash and interrupted him, saying: 'Ahah! So you've turned yourself inside out, have you? I'll soon have you the right way round.'

And he jumped on the drumikin, and with teeth and paws tore the inside out of it, and made himself a very good dinner.

Tiger, Brahman and Jackal

Hunting through the jungle one day, a tiger got himself caught in a trap. At first he was furious, roaring mightily and lashing the bars with teeth and claws; then, when this did no good, he wept and whined for his lost freedom.

Just then, along came a poor Brahman.

'Holy one,' called the tiger. 'Please save me, and let me out of this dreadful cage.'

'That would never do,' said the Brahman. 'If I let you out, you will surely eat me up.'

'Never!' said Tiger, and he swore a solemn oath. 'If you set me free, I will be your servant for ever.'

The wretched animal sobbed so miserably that the good Brahman's soft heart was touched, and at last he slipped the catch and opened the cage door.

Out jumped Tiger and grabbed him by the arm. 'What a fool you must be to trust a tiger. Now I've got you, do you think I am going to miss my chance of dinner? I'm starving.'

Plead as he might, the Brahman could not coax the tiger into sparing him. But the beast's sharp teeth sharpened his wits, and after many arguments he at last got the tiger to agree that they should put his case to three judges.

First the Brahman asked a pipal tree which was shading their path. 'It's no use complaining to me,' said the tree unsympathetically. 'Here I am, giving shelter to anyone who passes by, and all they do in return is tear off my branches to feed the cattle. Stop snivelling, Brahman, and take your fate like a man!'

That did not cheer the Brahman. Next he turned to a buffalo which was harnessed to a water-wheel. 'What a fool you must be,' said Buffalo, 'if you expect anyone to be grateful! Look at me! When I was a young cow and gave milk, they fed me on good cotton-seed and oil-cake. Now that my udders are dry, all I get is hard labour and short rations.'

In despair the Brahman turned to the road and asked for its opinion. 'Never expect anything but injustice!' said Road. 'Just take my case. I am helpful to everyone. Rich and poor, big and small, they all walk along me and I ease their travel. And what do I get in return? A kick in the face and the hot ashes from their pipes! No,' said Road. 'Only a fool looks for justice in the world.'

As his three judges had all ruled against him, the Brahman turned back sadly to give himself up to the tiger. Just then he came upon a jackal. This one said cheerfully: 'Why, whatever's the matter, holy one? You look as sick as three drowned kittens.'

The Brahman told him his story. 'I don't understand this,' said Jackal. 'It seems a mixed-up story. Tell me all over again.'

So the Brahman went through the whole thing again. 'No, it's no good,' said Jackal. 'I can't get things sorted out. Let's go back to where it all happened, and then it may be clearer.'

So they went back to the cage, where the tiger was standing, growling and sharpening his claws. 'You've taken your time,' he snarled at the Brahman. 'Come along, now. Dinner is served!'

'Yes,' thought the poor Brahman. 'But only one of us is sitting down to eat it!'

Hoping to live a few minutes longer, he turned pleadingly to the tiger and said: 'Just a few words, mighty one. I must explain something to this jackal who is a bit slow in his wits.'

'Very well,' growled the tiger. So the Brahman went slowly through the whole tale again, making it last as long as he could.

'Oh, my poor head!' cried Jackal. 'I can't get this sorted out. Start again. Now you, Brahman, were in the cage and Tiger came walking by . . .'

'No, you fool!' interrupted Tiger. 'I was the one in the cage.'

The jackal trembled with fright and with the effort to force his poor brain into understanding. 'Yes, of course,' he stammered. 'I've got it now. I was in the cage . . . that is to say, I wasn't, he was . . . oh dear! My weak wits! Let's see. The tiger was in the Brahman, and the cage walked by . . . That can't be right. I shall never get it clear. You had better start dinner.'

Tiger was maddened by the jackal's stupidity. 'I'll make you understand!' he roared in a fury. 'Now, see here. I am the tiger.'

'Yes, mighty one.'

'And that is the Brahman.'

'If you say so, mighty one.'

'And that is the cage.'

'I see, your excellency.'

'Right. Now I was in the cage. Have you got that?'

'Yes. . . . No . . . Not quite. If you please . . .'

'What is it?' said Tiger angrily.

'How did you get in?' asked Jackal.

'How did I get in? How do you think I got in, you fool? The usual way.'

'Dear oh dear!' said poor Jackal, still confused. 'Don't be angry with me, your worship. What is the usual way?'

At this Tiger was beside himself with impatience. He jumped up and bounded into the cage, shouting: 'This way! Now have you got it into your stupid head?'

'Yes,' said Jackal with a grin, and he slammed the door tight. 'I quite understand now. And it seems to me that we had better leave things as they are.'

The Story of Prince Sobur

There was a merchant who had seven daughters. He had done well in the way of business and was very wealthy.

One day he said to his daughters: 'Who do you depend on for your well-being?' The eldest daughter said: 'Why, on you, dear father.' All the others said the same, right up to the youngest. But the youngest daughter replied: 'I depend on myself, father.'

Instead of thinking what she meant, the merchant became angry and shouted: 'Ungrateful girl, don't you see that you depend on your father? Very well, try getting on without me. You can clear out of my house, and not a coin nor a scrap of food will you take with you.' And without another word he had his servants take her away.

The girl persuaded them to let her fetch her work-box, and then she climbed into her palki and the attendants carried her away. As they were trotting along, calling out the time so that they kept in step, an old woman ran out and called them to stop. 'Where are you taking my little girl?' she said, and the daughter saw that it was her old nurse. When the old woman heard what was happening she insisted on going too, so the servants, with much grumbling, let her climb into the chair and the two were carried away into the forest.

After several hours, when they had reached the heart of the jungle, the servants put down their burden and left the two women sitting on the ground beneath a very big tree. There was the poor girl, so gently brought up and never before exposed to any danger, now abandoned in the wild jungle and with no company other than an old and foolish woman. She could not help weeping a little at the thought of her plight. As she wept the big tree joined in and dropped a few tears on her. Then it said: 'You poor young girl, I grieve for you. Soon the wild animals will be coming out to hunt for their evening meal, and they are sure to catch you. But see! I will open up my trunk to make a crack. You and the old woman must squeeze inside and there you will be safe.'

So it did, and the two crept inside. Then the tree closed up again, leaving them in the dark. Soon the forest around them was full of the sounds of wild beasts. A tiger snarled, and there was the snuffling breathing of a big black bear. The wild boar grunted, and the earth shook under the tramp of elephant and buffalo. They all picked up the scent of the two women and came up to the great tree. They growled in fury as they found they could not reach their prey. In their anger they dug horns and claws into the tree-trunk and tore it grievously. They tore off great slabs of bark and broke away thick branches. But the tree stood firm and the two were quite safe inside.

It seemed a long night, but it passed at last. In the light of dawn the tree opened its door and the two women came out and stretched themselves. The animals were all gone, but the tree was sorely wounded. The merchant's daughter cried out in distress and said to the tree: 'Mother! How you have suffered for our sakes! You must be in agony.' And she went at once to a tank nearby and, scraping up wet mud, she plastered the tree with it.

'Thank you, my dear,' said the tree. 'That feels much better. Now, listen. There is no use in my saving you from the beasts if you are going to die of hunger. We must see about getting food. I have no fruit of my own. So give the old woman some money and tell her to go into the city nearby and buy food.'

But the girl had no money. She searched through her work-box, and all she could find were five cowrie shells. They were not much good, but the tree told the old woman, nevertheless, to take them to the city and buy some fried paddy.

The old woman wandered through the forest and at last came to a city. She went to the market and said to a food-merchant: 'Five cowries' worth of paddy, please.'

He laughed and said: 'Be off with you, granny! I don't work for charity.' She tried several other stalls, and at last found one with a kind-hearted tradesman in charge. He saw that she was in trouble, and old and tired too, so he took her cowries and gave her in exchange a big bag of paddy.

When she got back, the tree said: 'You must divide

the paddy into five heaps. You may eat one part now. Put three parts aside for the future, and scatter what is left on the sides of the tank.' They thought this was strange advice, but they did what they were told without arguing. The food tasted good, for they had not eaten for a whole day and night. After scattering the precious paddy in the forest, they prepared for another night of danger. The tree opened up its side and they climbed in. Then they lay in the dark while the wild beasts stormed outside and wounded the poor tree. What the women could not see was that other animals had come to the clearing, too. These were peacocks which arrived in huge numbers, attracted by the paddy. Although there was plenty of food they struggled for it, and as they fought their long tail feathers were torn out. In the morning, when the two came out of their tree, the ground was strewn far and wide with the gorgeous blue plumes.

The tree told the women to gather these feathers, and out of them the merchant's daughter made a wonderful fan. That day they took it to the city and offered it for sale at the palace. The young prince admired it greatly and readily paid a great deal of money for it.

Now the daughter's fortunes began to change. Every day she collected the feathers dropped in the night and these were sold in the market. In a short time the two women were rich.

'Good!' said the tree. 'Now it is time to find somewhere better than my trunk to sleep in! You must have a house built.' So they employed builders and set them to work to put up a fine house in a clearing of the forest. A beautiful garden was laid out around it, and a deep tank was dug to provide them with water.

While all this was going on, the merchant fell on bad times. Some of his enterprises failed and very soon he found that he had lost his fortune. So he had to sell his businesses, his house and his land, and he had to go, with his wife and six daughters, to try to find some way of making a small living. They wandered from town to town, picking up work where they could, and came at last to the place where a new house was being built. The merchant and his wife offered themselves to the foreman and were taken on to help dig the tank.

One morning the youngest daughter went to the site to see how the work was getting on. She stood watching the workmen, and suddenly she realised that two of those who were staggering under big loads were her mother and father.

The father whom she remembered as rich and dignified was now dirty and ragged and worn out with heavy labour. She called a servant and ordered him to bring the two workmen to her. When they received this summons they were frightened. It was the custom in those days to kill slaves and bury their bodies in the foundations when a palace was being built, and this, they feared, would be their fate. They were puzzled and even more afraid when they were made to take off their rags, bathe and put on fine robes. Then they were brought before the owner of the new house. When they found courage to look her in the eyes, they saw that it was the daughter whom they had injured. She held out her arms to show that they were forgiven, and they embraced and wept for joy. 'You were right, my dear,' said the father, 'when you said that you depended on yourself. You have proved it so.'

The daughter would not go home with them, for she had made her own life and so she would live it. But she gave her father a large sum of money from her fortune, so that he could set up in business once more. This he did, and he decided to go in for trade abroad. He bought a ship and loaded it with goods. Before sailing he asked his six daughters what they would like him to bring them from foreign parts. He thought it hardly worth asking the youngest daughter, for she was so rich that she must have everything she could wish, but at last he decided to ask her all the same. He therefore sent a messenger to her house. She was busy when the messenger arrived, so she said to him: 'Sobur', which means 'Wait a moment'. The servant, who was a foolish fellow, thought she meant that she wanted her father to bring home a 'Sobur' for her, so that is what he told the merchant.

The merchant now set sail, and he was away a long time, visiting many ports and doing good business. As he saw them he bought the gifts that his daughters wanted, but nowhere could he find a 'Sobur' for the youngest. He had no idea what it looked like, nor had any of the people he asked. At the last port of all he became anxious. Having failed in the market, he decided to shout his needs in the street, so he walked along calling: 'Wanted, a Sobur! Good price paid for a Sobur!'

Now it happened that the king's son in that country was called Sobur. The young man heard the cry and was amused and curious. So he made enquiries why the merchant was so anxious to buy a Sobur. Then he sent for the man who came quickly and bowed low before him.

'I understand that you want a Sobur for your daughter, good merchant,' said the prince. 'I have just the thing you want,' and he brought out a little box delicately carved in wood. Inside this was a fan with a little looking-glass set in it. 'Here is your Sobur,' he said. 'I trust that it will please your young daughter.'

The merchant joyfully took the toy and set sail for home. When he got back he distributed his presents, but the youngest daughter was busy as usual and put the box away without looking at it.

A few days afterwards, she happened to have a moment to spare, and she idly picked up the little box. She opened it and there was the fan. She took it out and shook it, and there, in the room with her stood Prince Sobur. 'Well, here I am,' he said. 'You called me and I came. What do you want with me?'

That was a surprise! When she got over the shock, the youngest daughter questioned the prince, and he told her how he had tricked her father into bringing the box and the fan. The magic of the fan was that, whenever it was shaken, the prince would appear. The truth was that both prince and merchant's daughter liked very much what they saw in one another. In a very short time indeed, they were well and deeply in love, and nothing would do but marriage without delay.

Now the prince went home to tell his father that he had found a wife, and the king was not dissatisfied with his choice. A day was fixed for the wedding, and of course the merchant and his wife and all six daughters were invited. But the sisters were bitterly jealous of the youngest's happiness and good fortune. They would not be content with anything less than the bridegroom's death. So they ground glass into a fine powder and spread it in the bridal bed. The prince lay down, suspecting nothing. In a few minutes he began to feel uncomfortable; a little longer and he was in great pain. The glass worked itself into every pore so that he screamed in agony. His attendants suspected treason, and at once they snatched him up and rushed with him back to his own country, where not even all the wisest doctors in the kingdom could relieve him of his suffering. So he lay in pain for many days.

But what about his bride?

The young girl was overwhelmed with grief at the sudden loss of her husband. She was not one to sit around weeping, however, and very soon she made up her mind to find him and somehow bring him back to health. There was a long and dangerous journey before her, and no girl could hope to make it unharmed. So she decided to disguise herself as a sannyasi, a holy beggar whom no one would dream of hurting.

She stripped herself of her fine clothes and put on a few rags, tied her hair into a knot and wound a pugri about it. Barefoot and armed only with a dagger, she set out on the road. Most of her life she had been wealthy and had lived at ease, and she was not used to the hard life of the traveller. Soon her feet were bleeding and she was very weary. After a while she sat down under a tree to rest. She noticed that there was a big bird's nest in the tree, and two enormous birds flew away as she settled at the foot. Now these were sacred birds, and they had gone to hunt for food for their young in the nest. Suddenly the chicks started to screech, and the girl saw a serpent climbing the tree to attack them. At once she drew her dagger and cut the snake in two. When the parent birds returned, their children told them how the young beggar had saved their lives.

The father bird said: 'I wish we could do him some service in return.'

His mate replied: 'Perhaps we can. Don't you see that it is no man who lies down there but a girl? She is the new bride of Prince Sobur, who even now is dying with glass in his body. She has risked her life to seek him out and cure him.'

'But how can she do this?'

'Quite easily,' said the mother bird. 'If she gathers up the dried droppings that lie around our nest, she can make them into a powder which can be brushed into the prince's body, mixed with milk and water, seven times a day. Without doubt this will make him well.'

'But she will never get there in time. She is only a weak girl and it will take her weeks to walk all the way. Surely the prince will be dead before she arrives.'

'That is where we can help,' said the mate. 'If we fly together, we will surely be strong enough to carry her there and back again. But she must take no pay for her services or all will be lost.'

Down below the girl had been listening eagerly to every word which the birds spoke. Now she stood up and called to them, agreeing to all their proposals. So, following their instructions, she gathered up the droppings, and then held on tightly to the great birds. They flew through the air with great speed, and soon she was put down in the courtyard of the king's palace.

She told the guards that she was a famous healer come to help relieve the prince of his pain. She was taken to the king, who had no great hopes of her but agreed to give her a chance. She ordered the servants to bring vast quantities of milk and water. She made a paste of this with the droppings and, with a long feather, she carefully brushed this over the prince's body, making sure that it went into every pore. Seven times she carried out this operation. Each time the prince's pain became less, and after the last application he sat up in bed and said that he felt quite well.

The king and queen and all the court were

delighted. They praised the beggar-healer to the skies, and the king ordered the riches of his treasury to be laid before him in payment. But the disguised girl would take nothing. All she asked was a plain gold ring from the prince's finger, so that she might remember him by it. This was readily given, and she quickly left the palace. In a quiet clearing the two sacred birds flew down, and in a few moments they had brought her back to their nest.

She felt so happy that the walk home seemed quite short. She slept well that night, and in the morning she took out the little box. There lay the magic fan. She picked it up and shook it, and Prince Sobur stood before her. He rejoiced to see his bride again, and he was full of amazement when she showed him the ring from his own finger on hers. So this was the healer who had saved his life. Nothing now stood between them and many years of happiness.

Camel gets his own Back

You would never have thought that the camel and the jackal would get on well together, but there it was. They were the best of friends.

One morning the jackal said: 'I'll tell you what we'll do today. Over the river I know where there is a very nice field of sugar-cane, just the kind of treat you would fancy. If you take me across the river I'll lead you there. While you are eating the cane, I will root about on the river-bank for crabs and fish-bones and I'll be sure to get a good dinner.'

The camel agreed. He knelt down and let the jackal climb on his back. Then he waded into the river and swam across very easily. The camel settled down to enjoy his sugar-cane, while the jackal ran up and down the bank, finding plenty of fishy scraps to gobble.

His belly was much smaller than the camel's, and so he was satisfied quite soon while the camel was only just beginning his meal. No sooner had he finished eating than the jackal began racing around the field, yelping at the top of his loud voice.

'Hear that!' said the villagers. 'There's a jackal in the sugar field. He will tear holes in the ground and ruin the plants.' So they snatched up sticks and ran off to the field. When they got there, what they saw was not the jackal but the camel, calmly gnawing the canes and sucking out the sugar. They shouted and yelled and whacked the poor camel until he howled just as loudly. By the time they stopped he was half dead from his beating.

At last they gave up and went back to their work. 'Come on,' said the jackal; 'we'd best go home.'

The camel limped to the water, and knelt down. 'Jump up,' he said, and the jackal scrambled on his back again. The camel swam into midstream, then he trod water and said: 'You're a fine friend to have, jackal. You made a good meal yourself and then spoilt mine. Why did you have to make such a din and draw the villagers down on me like a swarm of bees? Goodness knows, they stung like bees too!'

'Sorry!' said the jackal. 'I just couldn't help it. It's my habit to sing a song or two after dinner.'

So the camel swam on. He was in deep water now. He looked back at the jackal and said: 'You know, it's a funny thing. I feel the most tremendous urge to roll.'

'Don't do that!' said the jackal. 'Whyever should you want to?'

'Oh, I don't know. It's just a habit I have. I always have a little roll after dinner.'

Then the camel rolled once, twice, three times. The jackal was shaken off into the water and quickly disappeared. So the camel swam to land and went quietly to bed.

An Ambitious Mouse

A holy man had set up house on the banks of the sacred river Ganges. All day he sat thinking deeply about God and the need for virtue. His only shelter was a hut which he had plaited with palm leaves, and there he ate his supper and slept for an hour or two each night.

He lived all alone, for the nearest village was many miles away. But not quite alone. When he cooked his simple meal, a little mouse would creep out of the wall and sit by his side. The good man would not have hurt his worst enemy for all the world, and the animal had no fear of him. So it would pick up the crumbs as they fell from his hands and afterwards would kiss his feet in gratitude for the meal.

The holy one grew fond of his little companion and often spared a few minutes to play with it. Then, being lonely, one day he gave the mouse the power of speech and they talked together of simple things.

One day the mouse came to him, bowed and touched its forehead with its forepaws in reverence. 'Master,' it said. 'You have been very good to me. Will it anger you if I ask a favour?'

'Ask on, little mouse,' said the wise man.

'When you go in the morning to pray by the river,' said the mouse, 'a cat comes into our hut and chases me. I really believe that if it were not for the feeling of goodness which you leave behind she would have eaten me up long ago. One day she will forget herself, and that will be the end of me. If I became a cat I should have nothing to fear.'

'Why not!' said the holy man. So he took water, blessed it, and threw it over the mouse. At once it became a fine fat lady cat.

A few days went by. Then, in the quiet evening hour the wise man said: 'Well, my puss! How do you like your new life?'

'Not a lot!' said the cat.

'Why, whatever is wrong?'

'Your holiness has made me a strong cat,' she said. 'I could keep my end up against any other cat in the world. But now I have another enemy. When you go out in the morning to pray, a pack of noisy dogs comes along and scares the breath out of my body. I just can't stand it! Please, your goodness, make me a dog.'

'Very well, be a dog!' And so she was, the biggest, noisiest, most bouncy bitch you could imagine.

So the days passed. Then, one evening, the dog came and said: 'You have been kinder than I deserve. You made me a cat and now a dog. But a dog's life is not all fun. You have given me such a big body and a big stomach to go with it, but I still have to live on the scraps from your table. It just isn't enough. I am always hungry. Just look at the apes in that tree. They spend the whole day gathering fruit and eating their fill. If only I were an ape. That would be happiness!'

'If that is really what you want, be an ape!' And the dog became a fine lady ape, hairy and agile, and she went jumping for joy through the trees.

Summer was coming, and it grew hotter and hotter. The pools in the forest dried up to nothing, and even the great river shrank so that the ape found it hard to reach the water. She watched a herd of wild boars splashing in the mud and rolling in it. 'That is the life for me!' she said to herself. 'What pleasure to feel the cool mud creeping into every pore!'

She went and told the holy man of her ambition. He smiled at her words, but it was not his way to deny a friend anything. So he blessed the ape and she became a wild sow.

How she enjoyed the next few days! She lay and wallowed in the mud all day and could not get enough of it. But one morning the king came hunting. He came thundering through the forest on a splendid elephant, all hung with cloth-of-gold. The herd scattered and the king followed one of the big boars until he was out of sight. What splendour! thought the sow. It must be wonderful beyond any words to carry a king on your back, and to be decked in such finery. Just think! To serve a king!

So she went back to her old friend and told him what she wanted.

'Even I cannot make you a royal elephant,' he said. 'What I will do is to make you into a most beautiful wild elephant, and the rest is up to you.' So he did this, and she wandered through the jungle, trumpeting and making the earth shake with her mighty step. It was not long before the king's men saw her. They could see that she was fine beyond the ordinary, and they soon decided to add her to the king's team. She of course was not unwilling, and very soon she had been caught and led into captivity in the royal stables.

She quickly learnt how to carry passengers and

became one of the king's principal mounts. A few days later the queen decided that she wanted to go and bathe in the holy river. The king ordered the new elephant to be brought and saddled; then the king and the queen mounted on her back.

That is where the trouble began. The elephant was proud. She was glad to serve the king, but she did not believe that the queen, being a woman, was any better than herself. It was a disgrace to have to carry her. So she threw up her trunk and squealed loudly. Then she upped with her back legs, a strap broke, and the queen was thrown on to the ground. Down jumped the king and took her in his arms, kissing her and crying out in his distress.

Meanwhile the elephant ran off into the forest, for she knew she had been wicked and would be punished. As she ran, she thought about what had happened. What a thing it is to be a queen! she thought. Even the king kneels to her and kisses the dust from her face. It must be the best thing of all to be a queen.

With this in her mind she went home to find her holy man. Sure enough, there he was praying as usual. She told him what she wanted. The holy man smiled gently. 'What a silly child you are!' he said. 'How can I turn you into a queen? They only become queens by marrying kings! But I will do what I can. I will make you into the most beautiful girl in the world, full of goodness of heart and with the best of manners. Then, if you can find a king, you will have a good chance of pleasing him.'

The holy man took water again and threw it over the great beast. She shivered as the water touched her, seemed to shrink into herself, and there stood the most beautiful young girl. He kissed her brow, blessed her, and gave her the name of Postomani (which means Poppy-seed).

Postomani would not leave the good old man but stayed with him, keeping the hut clean and caring for the garden. She was sitting alone outside the door one day when a richly-dressed man came past. He had been hunting and had lost his way. She invited him to take refreshment, and he gladly entered and sat down.

Before fetching the food, Postomani brought water and knelt to wash her guest's feet. He checked her, saying; 'That is not right. It is true that I am the king, but I am of the warrior caste and you must be Brahmani, for I see that you are a holy man's child.'

'Not so,' said the girl. 'I am only an adopted child. Indeed I believe that my parents were, like you, Kshatriyas. So I can obey the laws of hospitality and wash you.'

So she did, and then brought him water and fruit. As he ate, she told him that she was the daughter of a king who had been killed by wild animals. She had been taken to the holy man's hut and brought up by him.

The king listened to this story—which we know was not true—with great excitement. Very soon he was over ears in love with the beautiful girl and would not be satisfied until she promised to be his wife. As you may imagine, she was not unwilling, and the holy man, coming home at that moment from his prayers, readily agreed to perform the marriage ceremony.

So the girl became a queen. She was carried off to the palace where the king could not give her enough treasures, so great was his love for her. She lay on silk cushions all day and the king's other wives waited on her hand and foot.

This happiness could not last. She went to bathe in

the palace tank one day. As she stood on the edge of the water she was taken with dizziness and fell, hitting her head. Before anyone could come to her help she had drowned.

The king was overcome with grief. He neglected all care of his kingdom and sat every day in tears. News of the sad event came to the holy man, and at once he made his way to the palace. To the sorrowful king he said: 'Do not grieve. You cannot change fate. Your dear queen was not of royal blood. She was a mouse, I befriended her, and at her whim I turned her into a cat, a dog, an ape, a boar, an elephant and a girl. She has gone now and you cannot have her back. But you need not forget her. We will make her name immortal. Bury her body among the flowers in your garden— for, not being human, she could not be burned as a Hindu—and out of her grave will grow a tree. We will call it Posto, after her. It will be the poppy-tree, and out of it men will make a powerful drug called opium. When they eat it, men will take one quality from each of the creatures which made up your queen, Postomani. They will be cheeky as a mouse, greedy as a cat, bad-tempered as a dog, dirty as an ape, savage as a boar, proud as an elephant, and high-spirited as a queen.'

And so it was.

A Pot-full of Daydreams

There was once a Brahman and a right mean one he was too.

He had been out begging all day and had collected a big load of rice. Even after he had eaten his dinner, there was enough left over to fill a pot. He hung this pot up by its handle on the wall above his bed. Then he lay down but could not sleep for thinking about all that beautiful rice.

He thought to himself: Just look at the fine rice. Was there ever a better pot of goodness? Now, just suppose there was a famine; why, I could sell the rice in the market and make a hundred rupees on it. A hundred rupees! That would buy a pair of goats. Let's see now; if they had kids twice a year, I could build up a herd in a few years. Now I think I will sell the goats and get cows. When the cows have calved, I will sell the calves and buy buffaloes with the money. Now, where shall

we go from there? I think I will buy mares with the buffalo money. That will soon give me a great many horses; I will sell them for cash and have a big hoard of gold. I will put that into property and get myself a fine house.

When I am in my house a rich Brahman will come to call. When he sees what a catch I am, he will offer me his lovely daughter and a big dowry too. Soon we will have a son. I shall call him Somasarman. In a year or two he will like dancing on my knee. I shall be sitting reading, and the boy will jump off his mother's lap and come running to be danced on my knee. I will be too busy and will call to my wife: 'Take the baby, woman! Take him!' But she will be thinking about preparing dinner and will take no notice. So up I shall jump and give her such a kick.

At this point the Brahman kicked out wildly, caught the pot and smashed it into pieces. Down came a shower of rice which turned him white all over.

And nowadays, when anyone goes in for wild daydreams, people call him 'Somasarman's Daddy'.

Bagging the Ghost

There was a young barber, and a good barber he was too, but he had married a wife. She nagged him day and night. 'Why did I leave my home and my dear father for such as you?' she would say. 'I never knew when I was well off. I went to bed with a full belly every night in those good days, not like now when I rarely manage to eat my fill. What right have you to marry a well-brought-up girl if you can't afford to feed her? I might as well be a beggar or a widow.' And so on.

The poor barber bore it all patiently but he did not

like it. Then, one day, having worked herself up into a right frenzy with her grumbling, the wife picked up the broomstick and gave him a big whack with it.

That was too much. He picked up the bag in which he kept the tools of his trade, slung it over his back and walked out of the house, swearing that he would not come back until he had made his fortune. That gave his scold of a wife something to cry about!

The barber wandered on from village to village, picking up a few pice here and there by shaving or hair-cutting. In time it began to get dark, and he found himself in a great forest. He could not see to go on, so he threw himself down at the foot of a big tree and brooded over his troubles.

Now in India, in many a big tree there lives a ghost, and this was one of them. Tree-ghosts are nasty creatures who make a living by jumping on passers-by and sucking their blood, and this tree had one of the nastiest of the whole tribe. The ghost saw the dim form of the barber and at once floated down. 'Aha, a barber!' it said. 'Just what I fancy! Prepare yourself, for I am going to kill you. There's no escape!'

Well, of course the barber was terrified. He was a sensible fellow, however, and even in this crisis he kept his head. He looked up boldly at the ghost and said in a cheerful voice: 'A ghost! Just what I wanted! I've been collecting them all day, and I want just one more to bring my bag up to a dozen.'

He stretched over to his tool-bag, fumbled in it, and brought out a looking-glass which he kept to show his customers how well he had shaved them. Standing up, he shoved the glass right into the ghost's face and said: 'Take a look at that! Here's one of your clan that I caught just an hour ago, and now I've got him safely bagged.'

The ghost saw itself in the mirror and believed what the barber told him. At once he fell into a panic. 'Oh, sir!' he whined. 'Please don't bag me. I couldn't bear that. I'll give you anything you ask if you let me go free.'

'I know you ghosts,' said the barber. 'One can't trust any of you. You promise anything, but if I let you go I'll not see you again.'

'Believe me,' said the ghost. 'I promise, ghost's honour! Anything you want, I'll get right away.'

'Very well,' said the barber. 'I'll trust you this once. But if you let me down, into the bag you go and no escape! Now listen; what I want is this. First, fetch me a thousand pieces of gold right away. Then you must build a barn next to my house and fill it to the rafters with paddy. Off you go now, and don't forget; fail me, and it's the bag for you!'

Trembling and promising with many oaths, the ghost went away. In a very short time he was back, carrying a huge sack full of gold coins. Then he went away again to start building.

The barber staggered home with the sack of gold over his back. He banged on the door of his house. His wife was lying in bed, weeping for loneliness and bitterly repenting that she had beaten her husband. She came to the door, and the barber poured a stream of gold at her feet. Well, you can imagine what she thought about that!

They heard a sound of knocking outside, and there was the ghost, hammering away at the new barn. He toiled away, still terrified at the thought of being bagged, and before noon the barn was finished. Then the ghost carried sack after sack of fine paddy until the barn was filled. It was dark before he had finished.

As the ghost staggered along under his last load he

met his uncle, who was just starting out for the night's haunting. 'What do you think you are up to, nephew?' he shouted. The ghost explained what had happened. 'What a fool you are!' said uncle. 'The barber must have tricked you. Do you think a feeble creature like he could bag a fully grown ghost?'

'You haven't seen him. He's the very devil of a barber.'

So they went together to the barber's house. Uncle crept up to the window and peered inside. As he did so, the cold wind which goes with ghosts everywhere blew through the house and woke the barber. At once he guessed what was happening. He grabbed his mirror and stuck it against the window, shouting: 'Come on! Here's another for the bag!'

Uncle saw himself in the glass and was just as frightened as his nephew. He threw himself on the barber's mercy, and agreed to build another barn, this time filled with rice. He carried out his task the very next day, and then escaped to the forest, thankful that he had not been bagged.

So there was our barber, a wealthy man after just two days. His wife quickly changed her old tune. Her belly filled every day with good food, she became very sweet and loving, and the barber, free of the need to ply his old trade, settled down to the business of raising a big and happy family.

A Devout Brahman

There was once a Brahman who was as poor as he was good. However willing he might be to work, he could not perform marriage or funeral ceremonies unless there were brides or bodies needing his service, and there were few rich people in his village to give him some of their plenty. So he and his family often went hungry and always ragged, and every day his wife made up in sharpness of tongue for her lack of food.

Still he did not forget his duty to the gods and he prayed long and tirelessly. Especially he poured out his prayers to Durga, his own particular patroness among the gods, and whenever his sufferings grew bitter he cried aloud to her: 'Durga! Oh Durga! Have mercy!'

One day, brooding over his troubles, he wandered far into the forest. There he lay down on a bed of leaves and cried out: 'Durga! Hear me, and answer my prayer. It is not for myself that I call, but for my wife and my children who are dying in misery. Help them by helping me to support them, I pray.'

Now it happened that Durga was walking nearby with her husband, the great god Shiva. They were very happy together, and in her contentment the goddess was moved to pity by the wretchedness of her servant. She said to Shiva: 'Do you hear that poor man? Every day he prays to me for hours on end. I almost weary of hearing him. Don't you think that we should do something to improve his lot? What he seems to need most is food.'

'That is a kind thought, my love,' said Shiva. 'Let us give him an ever-full vessel. That is usually a very welcome gift, and when he has it he may bother you less often.'

'An excellent idea!' said Durga. She at once sent one of her handmaidens for a cooking-pot, and when she had this she murmured words over it and then called the Brahman to her side. He came quickly and fell on his face before her.

'Get up, man!' she said. 'I know you are a good man and a kind husband and father. I shall now reward you. Take this pot. Every time you up-end it, out will come a stream of the finest paddy. You and your family need never go hungry as long as you keep the pot safe. And you can always sell what you have left over in the market.'

Not waiting for the Brahman's thanks, the goddess went back to her husband and they continued their walk. Excited beyond words the joyful Brahman hurried on his way. He had not gone far before he was tempted to try out his new treasure. So he stopped, turned the pot over and out flowed a great quantity of rich paddy. He scooped it up and tied it into a corner of his dress, and walked on homeward. The smell of the good food made him feel very hungry. It was dinner-time, but he could not eat until he had washed and said his prayers.

He came up to a wayside inn where there was a tank in which he could bathe. Before he went into the water he gave his precious pot into the safe-keeping of the innkeeper, telling him to take the greatest care of it.

The innkeeper thought it strange to make so much fuss about a very ordinary cheap pot. Directly the Brahman was out of the way, he decided to have a close look at it. He peered inside, but the vessel was empty. Strange, he thought. What's so important about an empty pot? He picked it up and, in order to examine it underneath, he turned it upside-down. Out came a torrent of the tastiest paddy. The innkeeper shouted for his wife, and she and her children came running. They fetched pots and jars and filled them with the precious food.

Here's a find! thought the innkeeper. I mustn't let this slip out of my hands. So he looked around for another pot which looked exactly like the Brahman's one, and switched the two vessels.

Now here comes the Brahman, soaking wet from his bath and reciting the holy scriptures as he comes. How hungry he is! And how good the paddy tastes when he takes it from the corner of his robe! It is a long time since he last ate his fill, and he enjoys every mouthful.

It was time to go home to share his good fortune with his family. The Brahman called for the innkeeper and asked for his pot. The landlord brought out a pot and placed it carefully into his hand, saying: 'There it is, your holiness, just as you gave it to me. No other hands have touched it.'

The journey home seemed short, so happy was the good man and so contented his thoughts. At the house he called his family to him, saying: 'See now; here is an end to all our sufferings. The gods have heard my prayers, and have given me a pot from which we shall find food as long as we live.' So saying, he raised the pot solemnly on high and turned it over. Out came nothing at all!

The Brahman's wife's low opinion of her husband took a turn for the worse. 'You holy idiot!' she shouted. 'Is this how you provide for your poor family? The gods must have sent you mad.' The poor wretched Brahman could do nothing but turn his pot over and over, but with no result.

'It must be that innkeeper,' he said at last. 'He must have tricked me.' And he went back and accused the man of exchanging the pots. The innkeeper put on a show of innocence and anger, and threw the Brahman out of his house.

Next day the Brahman went back to the forest, and prayed aloud to Durga to help him again. The goddess heard him and came to ask what had happened. She was annoyed at the Brahman's carelessness, but she was moved by his wretchedness and agreed to help him again. She sent for another pot and handed it to him without a word. Grateful and joyful he took it and went on his way.

Very soon he decided to try it. Lifting it high, he turned the pot over. Out came a stream, not of paddy but of demons. They turned on him and punched him and pinched him until he was covered with bruises. At last he thought to turn the pot the right way up and the demons disappeared into it.

Well, he thought. Here's a good present for my friend the innkeeper! So he went along to the inn and, just as he had the day before, he asked that man to take care of his pot. Then he went off to the bath. The innkeeper sent his wife and children for all the containers in the house. 'We're in luck,' he shouted. 'Perhaps it will be sweets this time.' Then he turned up the pot. Out came the demons who beat him and his family most cruelly. When they had done enough, they started on the house, and they would have wrecked it completely if the Brahman had not come back to see how things were going. He realised that the innkeeper had had enough, so he turned back the pot and sent the demons home.

'I'll take my first pot now,' he said firmly, and the innkeeper gave it back without a word. So the

Brahman went home, and this time his family were able to rejoice with him, for never had anyone had so rich a source of good food. Every day enough paddy was taken out of the pot to satisfy even the greediest of his children, and what was left over was sold. Very soon the Brahman had become the most famous food-merchant in the land; he was rich and built himself a fine house.

One day the youngest son, whose turn it was to draw out the day's supply of paddy, picked up the wrong pot by mistake and poured out a stream of demons. After this, the Brahman had this pot locked up and he alone kept a key.

So life went on happily for many days. Then, one day when the Brahman and his wife were both away at the market, the children began quarrelling as to whose turn it was to make the wonderful pot work. They struggled among themselves to get a hand to it, it slipped, fell to the ground and broke into a hundred pieces.

When the Brahman came home, he whipped all the children until they were sore and he was tired, but this could not put the pot together again. Ashamed, he went back to the forest and called to Durga. She heard his cry and came. She looked grave when she heard his story, but she gave him another pot, warning him solemnly that this would be the last. He worshipped her gratefully and went home. There he turned up the pot and out came the most beautiful sweetmeat, all curds, honey and sugar. How the naughty children loved it! Now the Brahman became famous as the best confectioner in all India, and his goods were sold in the farthest corners of the land.

Not everyone is glad at another's happiness. Many men were jealous of the Brahman's success. Among these was the chief man of the Brahman's own village. This Zemindar made secret enquiries and discovered the source of the Brahman's wealth, the magic pot. He decided that he must have this for himself. He therefore announced the wedding of his eldest son, and ordered the Brahman to provide refreshments at the feast. So that these would be quite fresh the Brahman must bring his pot to the Zemindar's house. The good man was not happy about this, for he knew the official's greedy heart, but he could not refuse.

What a feast that was! Never had so many sweets been gobbled; never had so many guests been overcome with sickness through their own greed. Then, when all the guests had gone home, the Zemindar had the Brahman and his family thrown out with blows and insults.

The Brahman went home without a word. There he unlocked his secret room and took out the demon-pot. He took it back to the Zemindar's house and knocked on the door. The Zemindar's servants opened, and the Brahman walked into the hall and overturned his pot. The first demon to come out, a very big and ugly one, grabbed the Zemindar by the nose. The next caught his wife by her hair. In a few seconds the Zemindar's family and friends were all screaming as they were pummelled and pulled, and the grand house was in ruins.

'Mercy!' shouted the Zemindar. 'Let us go and we shall be your slaves for ever.' He was in a sorry state, and so was his poor wife. The Brahman did not wait long before deciding that enough was enough. The demons were driven back into their pot, and the Brahman collected his precious food-pot and went quietly home with it.

He was never again troubled by greedy neighbours,

but lived his life in comfort and good deeds, never forgetting, among all the busy days, to give thanks to Durga who had laid the foundation of his good fortune.

Singh Rajah and the Jackals

In the jungle lived a great lion. He was lord of all the wild animals of that country, and so they called him Singh Rajah.

Every day he would come out of his den, stand on a rock and give his deep and mighty roar. Then his people would tremble and run wildly from one place to another; and he would make his choice, kill his prey and eat well for dinner.

But this could not go on for ever. In time he had no subjects left alive in all the jungle except two little jackals, husband and wife. The poor creatures had a hard life, running and hiding and every minute in fear of their lives.

The little lady jackal said to her husband: 'Do you hear how the lion roars? He will surely catch us today.' But her man replied: 'Be brave. I will take care of you. Just a little more effort and we shall be safe.' And so she would find a bit more strength and run faster, and so they would get through another day.

The day came when the lion was right on their tails. The she-jackal cried to her husband: 'It is all up with us now, beloved. I am so afraid.' But he called to her: 'Cheer up; there is still hope. Follow me.'

And bless me if those two clever little jackals didn't walk straight up to the lion's den. He could hardly believe his eyes when he saw them coming. He roared most dreadfully and lashed his tail in rage. 'Come on, you wretched animals!' he shouted. 'You've kept me waiting too long. Come and be eaten!'

But the male jackal crept up to him and whined:
'Oh Lord King, don't be angry. We know you are our
master, and we would have come and done our duty

long ago. But the great king chased us and tried to eat us up, and so we ran away and hid.'

'What great king?' snarled Singh Rajah. 'There is no king in the jungle but me.'

'I'm afraid there is,' said the jackal. 'It is hard to believe, for you are very strong and fearful. Your very voice is death to us poor creatures. But you don't compare with the other king. Why, to him you are as feeble as we are to you. His face is a flame of fire, his voice is like thunder. No animal could stand against him.'

'It is a lie,' roared the lion. 'Take me to him at once, and I will destroy him.'

The little jackals led the way through the jungle to a distant clearing where there was a deep well. 'Look, lord!' they said. 'There he is!'

The great lion looked down at the distant water, and there he saw a lion's head looking up at him. He roared defiantly, and so did the lion down below. He shook his head so that his mane spread out like a great cloud. The other lion did the same. He showed his enormous sharp teeth. So did the other. Singh Rajah grew terribly angry at the other lion's defiance. At last he could stand it no longer; with a last roar he leapt down the well, and the other lion came to meet him. There was an enormous splash. The other lion disappeared, and there was Singh Rajah struggling in deep water.

The walls of the well were tall and steep. In no way could Singh Rajah struggle out, nor could he reach the two little jackals who peered down at him. Very soon his struggles ended and he sank. And the jackals danced round the well head, singing: 'Ay Ay! The king is dead! Ding-dong! The lion's gone! Ay Ay!'

And they ran back into the forest where they were now king and queen.

The Boy with the Moon on his Forehead

In a corner of the king's garden there stood a small cottage, and here lived the gardener. The gardener's daughter used to play in the garden with her friends, and as they danced and sang she often said to them: 'When I am married I shall have a son. He will be the most beautiful boy in all the world, and he will have the moon on his forehead and a star on his chin.' Then her friends would all laugh and tease her.

The king walked in the garden and he heard what the children were saying. This set him thinking. He had married four wives, and not one of them had given him a son. He must try again for the sake of getting an heir to the kingdom, and why shouldn't he marry the gardener's daughter? She was healthy enough and very pretty, and if she had the child she talked of this would make a fine prince. So the king went and talked to the gardener, and the result was that he married the man's daughter.

It was a grand wedding and everyone was happy, except the king's other wives. However, they said nothing. Within a year the new queen was expecting a baby. The older queens visited her every day and made much of her. They said: 'The king is away every day hunting. Suppose that your baby came while he was away; that would be very bad.'

That night the gardener's daughter said: 'My baby will not be long now. I am worried that you are away from the palace every day. How can I get in touch with you when the time comes?'

The king understood what was troubling her. So he gave her a little drum, and said: 'When you want me, just bang this drum. I shall hear it, however far away I may be, and I shall come to you at once.'

Next day the king went out hunting as usual. When he had been gone a few hours the old queens came to the gardener's daughter and said: 'Now is your chance to see if the drum works. Give it a good bang and see what happens.'

'No,' she said. 'I won't do that. I must not take the king from his hunting without good reason.'

'This is a good reason,' said the wives. 'How do you know that he can hear you if you don't test the drum? You must try it.'

She was not happy about it, but at last she did what they said. She had hardly stopped beating the drum when the king rushed in, panting.

'I came at once, my love,' he said. 'Is the baby here yet?'

'No,' said the queen. 'I just wanted to see if you would really come when I called.'

'Very well,' said the king. 'But don't call me again without cause, or I shall be very angry.'

Only two days later the queens asked her to try again. She refused, but they went on and on until she tired of saying no, so she banged the drum and the king came running. This time he was really angry. 'Twice you have made a fool of me,' he said. 'There won't be a third time. Call as much as you like, I will not come to you.' And he went back to his sport, leaving her in tears.

A day or two later the young queen felt the baby coming. She banged the drum as hard as she could, and the king heard it, but he said: 'She won't trick me again. Let her bang until she bursts.'

In her distress she called for the four old queens. They told her: 'There is a custom in this country. When a royal baby is to be born, the mother is blindfold so that she cannot see it.' Then they tied a handkerchief over her eyes, and she lay still and let them.

Before long, the gardener's daughter had a baby boy, and he was very beautiful, and he had the moon on his forehead and a star on his chin. The four queens took him away at once and said to the nurse: 'Keep the baby quiet so that his mother does not hear him. Then tonight you must make away with him; kill him or hide him, whichever you like, but his mother must not see him.' They gave her a large sum of money to keep her silent. Then the queens went back to the mother and put a large stone in bed with her.

Now it was time to take off the handkerchief. 'Look!' they said. 'Here is your son. Won't the king be pleased?' And they all laughed. The young queen wept, but what could she do?

The king came home that evening, and the old queens were not slow to show him his new heir. He was furious. He cursed the young queen and banished her from his sight, making her work in the palace kitchen where she had all the hardest work to do.

But what happened to the baby? The nurse could not disobey the queens, but she did not want to kill such a beautiful child. She put him in a box and carried him at night to a clearing in the jungle. Here she dug a hole, put the box in, and covered it with earth. Then she went back to the palace, unhappy but too afraid of the queens to do anything else.

Now the king had a favourite dog called Shankar.

He had overheard what the queens said to the nurse, so he followed her into the jungle. As soon as the woman had gone Shankar scraped away the earth and pulled out the box. He opened it, and there lay a beautiful baby. He at once determined to protect the boy. But how was he to keep him hidden from his enemies? Shankar swallowed the baby whole and so hid him in his belly.

The days went by for six months. Then Shankar went out at night and brought up the baby. He was still alive and growing fast. Shankar was delighted. He licked the baby clean and played with him for a time. Then he swallowed him again. He kept him inside for another six months. Then once more he went out at night and brought the boy up and played with him. The baby was now a year old and strong and beautiful.

One of the servants looked after Shankar. He had noticed that the dog was behaving strangely, and he followed him into the jungle and saw all that happened there. He went back to the palace and said to the four queens: 'You won't believe the wonder I have seen. The king's dog keeps a baby in his belly. It's the loveliest boy you ever saw, and it has the moon on its forehead and a star on its chin. Never did you see such a sight!'

This was bad news for the queens. Next time they saw the king they ran to him and said: 'Such a fright we have had! Your dog Shankar got into our room today and jumped all over us. He tore our clothes and nearly frightened us to death. Next time he may kill us.'

'Don't worry,' said the king. 'I will see to it.' And he ordered his servant to kill the animal next morning. But Shankar heard all this and said to himself: 'For myself I care not, but they must not kill the child.'

That night he went to the king's cow, who was called Suri, and told her his story. Suri readily agreed to look after the baby, so she swallowed the little prince.

Next day the servants took Shankar out and shot him, but the child was safe in Suri's belly. There he stayed for a year. Then Suri brought him out, found that he was healthy and still beautiful, played with him for a while, and then swallowed him again. And so another year went by. At the end of the year the boy, who was now three years old, was brought out into the air again. He had grown and his beauty was even greater than before. The cow took him back safely into her belly and returned to her stable.

But this time one of the herdsmen had seen what happened. Full of amazement he ran and told the queens what he had seen. They were afraid and angry to know that the boy was still alive. When they got over their shock they ran to the king, their clothes torn and their hair wild. 'What a dreadful day we have had!' they told him. 'The cow, Suri, attacked us while we were walking. She tore our clothes, as you can see, and we were lucky to escape with our lives.'

'No need to be afraid,' said the king. 'I will deal with her.'

Suri heard what had happened and realised that her days were numbered. Her first concern was for the boy. At night she went to the stables and talked to Katar, one of the king's horses which was said to be bad-tempered and quite untamable. He had never known a man on his back, and indeed everyone was afraid to go near him.

Suri told Katar her story, and the horse at once agreed to help. So Suri brought up the boy. Katar admired his beauty and swallowed him very carefully. The two animals then said farewell to one another, and in the morning Suri was taken out and shot.

After a year Katar thought it was time to take a look at his charge. He brought up the boy, and he was still very healthy. They played together for a time, and then the horse took the child back into safety. So yet another year went by. When Katar took another look the boy was five years old. He was well-grown, strong and more beautiful than ever. Again the two played together, before the horse put him back into his hiding-place.

This time a groom had watched the two at play. He ran to give his strange news to the queens. They were horrified and full of fear. They wept and tore their hair and altogether lost a taste for food. When the king came back from his day's hunting he had rarely seen them looking so miserable.

'Why, what is the matter, my dears?' he said.

'It's that wicked horse of yours,' they wept. 'That Katar! He broke out of his stable and jumped on us. He tore our clothes and put us in fear for our lives. We shall never be happy again.'

'Don't you worry,' said the king. 'I'll have him dealt with in the morning.'

The king knew that the horse was very strong and fierce. It would be beyond his servants to kill such a beast, so he ordered a troop of soldiers to the palace next morning. He armed himself and decided to lead the soldiers personally so that there could be no mistake.

Katar knew what was in store for him. But he was not ready to die quietly. He brought up the boy and said: 'Go into the harness-room and get a saddle and bridle. In the next room you will find some very fine clothes and weapons. Dress yourself in suitable robes and choose a sword and a gun. Then you must put the

saddle and bridle on me, and mount on my back.'

The boy did as he was told. The king gave the order for the attack to begin, and at that moment the stable-door burst open and out came Katar with an armed boy on his back. All the king had time to see was a blur of horse and boy. Then he was knocked down and his soldiers scattered. They fired wildly, but not one of them got a shot home on the target. They formed ranks again, feeling ashamed, and the king sent them home.

Katar galloped on until they were far from the palace. When it began to get dark he stopped and the two settled for the night under a tree. The horse grazed and the boy found some wild fruit to eat. Next day they went on until they came into another country. Here the horse stopped and the boy got down. 'Unsaddle me,' said Katar. 'Now take off your fine clothes and make a bundle of them with your weapons.' Then the horse gave him some plain clothes and made him dress himself in them. They hid the bundle in the tall grass.

'They may stay there until you need them again,' said Katar. 'Now we must make our living in the jungle while you grow to manhood.'

And that is what they did. The horse and the boy went hunting every day, and with what the boy caught and the horse grazed they had enough to eat. The boy grew tall and strong, and he seemed more beautiful every day. In time he was on the brink of manhood.

One day Katar said to him: 'Now we must part. I will stay here, and you can find me when you need me. You must go and find service with some worthy man.'

'But what can I do, my father?' said the boy. 'I have no skills. I shall be lost without you.'

'Don't be afraid,' said the horse. 'You will manage

very well, and I shall be on hand when you need me.
Now, before you go, twist my right ear.' The boy did
so, and the horse became a donkey. 'Good!' said the
donkey. 'Now twist your own right ear.' The boy
obeyed, and at once he became a poor ugly man.

He walked for a long time and at last met a grain
merchant. The man asked him his business. 'I am a
poor man looking for work,' said the boy.

'Good,' said the merchant. 'I am looking for a man,
and you will do very well. You shall be my servant.'

The merchant's house was close by the palace
where the king of that country lived. The boy stayed
there and did his work to his master's satisfaction.

One night it was very hot. The boy had worked hard
all day, but he was restless. He went outside and
wandered into the cool of the palace garden. Here he
sat down and began to sing to himself, a very lovely
song. The king's youngest daughter was lying in bed,
unable to sleep, and she heard the song. She got up
and threw a robe about her, and went out into the
garden.

'Who are you? Where do you come from?' she
asked the singing stranger.

He said not a word and just went on singing his sad
song.

'This is strange,' said the princess to herself. 'Who
can this common man be who will not speak to the
king's daughter?'

She went back to bed, but the same thing happened
the next night, and the next.

After he had worked the next day, the boy went into
the jungle to find his horse. He told Katar all that he
had done since they parted and about the princess.

'She asked me who I was, but I did not know what to
answer.'

'Next time, tell her that you are a poor man who came to her country to find work,' said Katar.

The next night he went out and sang his song again. The princess came to him quickly and said: 'Who are you? Where do you come from?'

The boy said: 'I am only a poor man. I came from far away to find work, and I am a servant of the grain merchant.'

At this she went back to bed, but the same thing happened on the next three nights.

Next day the princess went to her father and said: 'Father, it is time that I was married. But I must choose my own husband.'

The king thought that this was reasonable, so he wrote to all the neighbouring kings inviting them to send their sons as suitors to his court. But he made it clear that it would be his daughter's choice.

During the next few days many kings and princes began to arrive at the palace, and very splendid they were too. When they had all assembled, the king said: 'Tomorrow my daughter will make her choice. We shall go into the garden so that my daughter may walk among you and see you all.'

The morning came, and the garden was full of fine princes in fine clothes. The boy was there too, among the other servants who had come to watch what was happening.

The princess was dressed in the most gorgeous robes and jewels blazed in her hair, her ears and nose, her fingers and toes. She held a gold necklace in her hand. She was mounted on a great elephant which was painted all in blue. She rode around the garden and looked closely at all the suitors. Then she rode over to the servants and hung the necklace on the neck of the grain merchant's servant.

Everyone laughed. What a joke that was! Then they became angry and shouted: 'What folly this is! Throw that dirty boy out of the garden. How dare he bring his filth into the royal presence!'

The boy went and stood in a distant corner of the garden by himself. Again the princess rode around the garden on her elephant, and again she put the necklace on the boy in his shabby clothes. At this all the kings and princes went to lay hands on him, but the princess shouted: 'Beware! He is under my royal protection.' And she made him climb on to the elephant and sit beside her.

The suitors were still more angry at this. The king stood up and said: 'My daughter may choose a husband wherever she wishes. She has twice chosen this common man, and she shall have him.' And with that they all had to be content. The marriage followed with great splendour, and then the kings and princes went back to their own countries.

The princess was happy with her new husband, but her six older sisters, who had all married princes, mocked her for having chosen to marry such an ugly and poor fellow. The six princes went out hunting every day and they left their new brother-in-law behind. The youngest princess was sad that he should be left out of the sport, and she urged him to join the others in the chase.

Then one day he said: 'I think I shall take the air today.'

'Good!' she said. 'Take a horse from the stable.'

'No,' said the young man. 'I shall walk.' And he went into the jungle and sought out Katar. He told the horse the whole story, and said that his wife wished him to go hunting.

'So you shall,' said Katar. 'Twist my left ear.'

He did so, and Katar turned back into the fine, fierce horse. 'Now twist your own left ear,' he said; and the common man disappeared and in his place stood a fine young prince with the moon on his forehead and a star on his chin. He found the bundle of clothes and dressed himself in finery and took up his sword and gun. Then he mounted Katar and went hunting.

What a day's sport that was! Wherever he went he found game. By evening his bag was full and he made camp by a clear stream and put a haunch of deer on the fire to cook. Meanwhile the six princes were having a bad day. They could nowhere find game, neither bird nor beast, and they rode until they were tired and very hungry. At last they came to the place where their brother-in-law was camping, but in his fine clothes and with his newly recovered beauty none of them knew him.

They bowed deeply before him, for clearly he was some great prince. Then, because great hunger made them forget their best manners, they begged for food and drink. He asked who they were, and they told him. 'Very well,' he said. 'I'll make a deal with you. I will feed you if afterwards you do what I say.' They were so hungry that they agreed, and he put before them a fine meal. While they were eating he took six pice pieces and lay them in the ashes of the fire until they were very hot. When they had finished, he made them lie on the ground, face down, with their coats off their backs. Then he touched each of them in the middle of the back with the hot coins, so that a bright red mark was left on them. It hurt a good deal, but they were brave and thought it a small price for so good a dinner. Then they parted.

The young man waited until they were far ahead.

Then he rode slowly to the palace. He was stopped at the gate, for the guard did not know this fine young prince. He said: 'I am the husband of the youngest princess.'

'Nonsense!' the guard said. 'You are nothing like him.'

'That is who I am,' said the prince. 'Fetch the princess.'

She came and looked at him. 'I have never seen a more beautiful man,' she said; 'but you are not my husband.'

'I am,' he said. 'I served the grain merchant, and sang in your garden. You chose me from all the kings and princes, riding on your blue elephant and hanging a gold necklace on me. See, here it is!'

Then she had to accept him, and glad she was that she had married such a fine man. She took him to her father, and he marvelled at the change in his new son-in-law. He was gladly accepted into the king's court and everyone made much of him.

One day the court was full of princes and ministers and officials. The young prince said in a loud voice: 'There are six thieves here.'

'What's that?' said the king. 'Where are they? Show me the villains and I will hang them.'

'There they are,' said the prince, and he pointed to his six brothers-in-law. 'Take off their coats.'

The six princes had to take off their coats, and there on their backs were the brands of a thief. The six were ashamed, and everyone laughed at them, not least the young prince who remembered how they had mocked him when he seemed a poor and ugly man.

After that, the prince and his bride lived together in great contentment. But the young prince often thought about his own home. The horse had told him the whole story of his birth and strange upbringing, and he longed to see the mother he had never known.

His father-in-law agreed that he and his wife should pay a visit to the neighbouring kingdom, and gave him an escort of soldiers and also elephants to ride. They travelled in great state and made camp on a plain outside the city. The king sent a message welcoming them and inviting them to the palace, and when they got there everyone was lined up to meet them, including the king's four wicked wives.

The young prince rose to address the crowd, but first he looked around. Then he said to the king: 'Is everyone here?'

'Everyone,' said the king.

'That is not true. I do not see one who was the gardener's daughter and who became your queen.'

'Ah yes!' said the king. 'She is busy at her duties.' And he sent for her.

She came in her shabby working clothes and gazed at the beautiful young prince. He came and knelt to her, then raised her up, and ordered that she should be dressed in the finest robes. Soon she was back, and she looked lovelier still in her rich clothes and jewels. The prince knelt to her again, and sat beside her at table, offering her the best of the food. The four queens were very angry, for he had paid no attention to them, but they could do nothing.

The feasting went on for several days. Then one day the prince said to the king: 'Have you no son?'

'Alas, no,' said the king. 'I never had a child of my own.'

'Yes, you did,' said the prince. 'I am your son.'

'I wish it were so, but not one of my queens had any children.'

'That is not true,' said the prince. 'The gardener's

daughter had a son, but the four queens stole him away and left a stone in his place. Do you remember how you killed your dog Shankar and your cow Suri at their request. This was because the animals befriended me. Do you recognize my horse.'

'Yes,' said the king. 'I would know that horse anywhere. It is Katar, who was mine.'

'Do you remember the day when Katar was to be killed, and he rushed out of the stable with a boy on his back? That boy was me.'

Then the king could doubt no more, but gladly acknowledged the prince as his son. He kissed him and begged his forgiveness.

'Now,' he said, 'you must come and live with me and help rule my kingdom.'

'That I cannot do,' said the prince. 'I will not live in a country where wives are dishonoured and murderers go unpunished. I will live in my wife's father's kingdom.'

'I will do anything to keep you with me,' said the king humbly.

'Then banish your four wicked queens to the farthest corner of your kingdom, and bring your youngest wife back into favour.'

And that is what the king did. And the young prince and his wife went to live in the palace, and when, after many years, the king died, he ruled in his place, and a happy kingdom that was. I don't know who was the happiest one in it, the prince, or his lovely princess, or the gardener's daughter, or Katar, the horse who grew strong and fat on the finest grain that the country could provide.

A Tale of Two Goats

It was market-day, and a herd of goats was being driven to town to be sold. Among them were two, a Billy-goat and a Nanny-goat, who had never met before but who now found that they liked one another very well.

Billy said: 'Here's a fine time to meet up with someone as nice as you! You know what is going to happen. When we get to town we'll be put up for sale, and whoever buys us we shall be due for the knife. Whatever can we do?'

'We must escape on the way to market,' said Nanny.

'A good idea,' said Billy, 'but even if we manage it, what next? If we run back here, they'll just catch us, and the whole business will start all over again. And if we make for a strange village where no one knows us the men are sure to grab us; then we'll either be packed off to market or killed and eaten on the spot. It looks as if we are sunk, whatever we decide.'

There was a gloomy silence, then Nanny spoke up: 'Why run to a village anyway? Shouldn't we steer clear of humans altogether and run away into the jungle?'

'A fat lot of good that would be!' said Billy. 'The jungle is full of wild beasts, and they are likely to be no kinder to us than the men. We shall end up a bear's dinner or lining a tiger's stomach.'

'Isn't it worth trying?' said Nanny. 'This way we have just a small chance of surviving. If we go to market we have no hope at all.'

Billy saw that his companion was talking good sense, and so it was agreed.

The way to town passed through dense forest, and when trees hid them from their masters the two goats slipped into the undergrowth and ran for their lives. Wandering on, they came at last to a great tree with a hollow trunk, and there they set up house. The days went by happily, and in time Nanny had three fine kids.

One day the goat family was at home, and the young ones, being hungry, began to bleat loudly. The noise was heard by a prowling tiger who decided that his problem of what to eat that day had been solved. He made straight for the hollow tree, his mouth watering and his tail lashing.

'Here it comes!' said Billy-goat to his mate. 'The

good times couldn't last for ever.' Still, he was not going to give up without a struggle. So he shouted to the kids: 'Aren't you ever satisfied? You are the greediest children I have ever known. You've had five tigers, three bears and half a dozen buffaloes today, and still you howl for more. I think it is quite disgusting. However, I see another tiger heading this way. I'll kill just this one, and that is your lot. Not another mouthful shall you have till tomorrow.'

This brought the tiger up short. What kind of beasts can these be, he wondered, who feed their youngest on the fiercest animals in the jungle? I'd best beat a retreat as quick as I can. As he turned he heard the Billy-goat shouting: 'Now look what you have done! You've frightened that tiger. I shall have to chase him.' That was more than the tiger could stand. He bounded away at top speed, and took no rest until he was far away from the dreadful hollow tree.

As the tiger lay panting, Honuman, the big black-faced monkey, came swinging through the treetops. Seeing the tiger in distress he dropped down and asked what the trouble was. When he could get his breath, the tiger gasped: 'My goodness! I've had an escape today. I'll tell you all about it when I can.' And after panting and groaning some more, he at last managed to tell the whole story.

Honuman laughed heartily. 'What a clown you are, Tiger!' he said scornfully. 'That goat fooled you thoroughly. Don't you see, he was scared to death of you, and only told that pack of lies to get rid of you.'

The tiger was not convinced, but after some argument he at last agreed that what the monkey said might be true. He didn't fancy putting it to the test, but Honuman pressed him strongly, and promised to return to the hollow tree with him.

'It's all very well for you,' said the tiger. 'At the first sign of danger you can be up the nearest tree and away. I'll have to stay on the ground at the mercy of this monster.'

'Here's what we'll do,' said the monkey. 'Let us knot our tails together, and then we can go, if not hand in hand, at least tail in tail.'

'That is fair,' said the tiger. So the monkey made a good strong knot with his clever hands, and the two animals went through the forest side by side with their tails trailing behind.

Soon they came in sight of the hollow tree. The Billy-goat was keeping watch, and he was not too pleased to see the tiger back again and with company. Tiger is stupid enough for anything, he thought, but it won't be easy to fool Honuman. But he did not give up. When the two beasts were within hearing, he shouted: 'You are a lazy rascal, Hono! Didn't I pay you to bring me a day's food? A fat lot of good a single tiger will be for my hungry children! If you can't do better than that, I see I shall be forced to eat you too.'

The silly tiger believed that Honuman was working for the goat and had tricked him into this situation. At once he fell into a fine panic and turned to run away. The monkey was not in the least fooled by Billy-goat's cunning, so he continued to advance on the tree. So there were the two big animals, tied by the tail and pulling in opposite directions. First the tiger gained some ground, then Honuman won it back. They were both so strong that something had to give way. It was the tiger's tail. Suddenly it came out by the roots, and off shot a tail-less tiger into the jungle.

Released from his companion the monkey fell head-over-heels. When he picked himself up he was startled to find that he now had two tails. He went off, jumping into the thickest bushes to rid himself of the strange tail but without success. All the other animals, who had long been bullied by him, jeered at him and made fun of his clumsiness, until he went to hide himself in the farthest corner of the forest. The tail-less tiger came in for his share of insults, and he too was forced into exile.

Danger had passed, for the time at least, and Billy and Nanny were able to get on with the business of bringing up their fine and hungry kids.

The Fakir Who Wanted to be Perfect

The king had no son to inherit his kingdom, and he and the queen were very sad. One day a holy beggar came to the palace and said: 'With my help the queen will bear twin sons. I will do my part if you promise to let me have one of the babies and keep just one for yourself.'

The king did not like the bargain, but one son was better than none, and so he agreed. The fakir gave him a flask of liquid which the queen must drink. Then he went away.

The queen took her medicine, and nine months later she gave birth to fine twin boys. As they grew they became ever more handsome and more dear to their parents. At first the king worried about his promise to the fakir, but as the years went by he thought of this less and less.

The man must be dead by now, or surely he would have claimed his part of the bargain.

The princes grew fast. They were good at their classes and good too with horse and hound, with bow and spear. Everyone loved them, and to their parents they gave the greatest joy.

Then they were sixteen, tall and straight. On their birthday a knock came at the palace gate, and it was the fakir. He demanded his share of the old bargain. You may imagine how the king and the queen felt! But they dare not deny the man his rights. Not only was the king's honour at stake; who knew what powers the holy man might have? Maybe he could call down curses on the land, or destroy the whole of the royal family.

One of the boys must go; but which one? Each was equally dear to the parents. And both of them were bold lads, ready for adventure and willing enough to go with the man. In the end it was agreed that the elder prince (if only by a minute or two) should go with the fakir.

Before he left, the boy planted a tree in the palace garden and said: 'This tree is my life. So long as it is green I am alive and well. If it turns yellow I shall be ill or in danger. If it turns brown I shall be dead.' Then he kissed his parents and his brother, and stepped out bravely with the beggar.

As they went on their way they passed a bitch with a litter of puppies. One of the pups said: 'Mother, that is a fine young man. He must be a prince. I will go with him.' The bitch agreed, and so the puppy ran after the boy.

In a short while they came to a tree in which a hawk had its nest and was rearing her young. One of the young hawks said: 'Mother, that is a fine young man. He must surely be a prince. I want to serve him.' The mother hawk agreed, and the young one flew down and perched on his wrist.

So the four travelled on deep into the forest, until they came to a lonely hut thatched with leaves. The fakir said: 'This is your home. Your work will be to gather flowers from which I make my drugs. You may eat what you like, and drink what you like. You may go anywhere to east, south and west, but to the north you must not go. Now, be about your business.'

The prince was not unhappy. The work was not hard, and he enjoyed searching the forest for rare plants. In his spare time, and there was plenty of it, he went hunting with his dog and his hawk. Best of all he loved to chase the big fat deer, and many a juicy hind

he carried back to the hut—but the fakir would have none of it.

One day the prince hunted deep into the forest and there wounded a big stag. The poor beast, sorely hurt, turned to the north to escape the hunter, and the boy, forgetting the fakir's warning, followed him closely. The stag ran up to a fine house and in through the door, and the prince followed. Inside, he found to his surprise not a stag but a very beautiful woman, who bade him welcome. He was greatly taken by her beauty, and when she suggested a game of dice he readily agreed.

The first stake was a dog. They threw, and the lady won. So she took the prince's dog and put it into a hole in the ground, blocking the end with a plank. Next they threw for a hawk. The lady won again, and the hawk was forced into another hole. The next stake was a man. They threw their dice a third time, and still the lady won. So the prince had to crawl into a hole in the ground, and the light was blocked out by a plank.

In the king's palace, the younger brother had visited his brother's tree daily and had rejoiced to see that it was bright green. Now suddenly it turned yellow and limp. He ran and told the king and queen, and they came to look. They knew at once that the elder prince was in danger. The young prince did not take long to decide that he must try to find and rescue his brother. He too planted a tree in the garden, and then he took a fast horse and rode off blindly into the forest.

Soon he passed a litter of puppies, and one of them insisted on joining him, saying: 'You took my brother. Take me too.' (For the brothers looked exactly alike.) The prince knew that he was on the right track. Soon he came to the hawk's nest, and a young hawk flew to

his wrist, saying: 'You took my brother. Take me too.'
So he rode on and came at last to the fakir's hut. No
one was about, and he could not guess where his
brother might be. He could do nothing but wait, and
this he did, although most impatiently.

At sundown the fakir returned. He said: 'Good! I
hoped that you would come. Your foolish brother
must have disobeyed me. I told him never to go to the
north, but he must have done so. A Rakshasi lives there.
Outwardly she is a beautiful woman, but she lies in wait
for men, and when she catches them she eats them.
Perhaps he has already made a meal for her.'

The young prince did not wait for morning, but rode
at once to the north. In the early light he saw a stag and
fired an arrow at it. Then he followed the wounded
beast until it went into the house. He followed, and
there sat the beautiful lady. He had seen no one lovelier,
but he was not deceived, knowing her to be a monster
under her disguise.

The lady proposed a game of dice and the prince
agreed. They threw, and the prince won. The lady
lifted a plank, and out ran the puppy, tail wagging,
and pranced about joyfully with his brother. They
threw again, and again the prince was the winner. She
released the hawk which rejoiced to meet its brother
again. They played once more, and again the prince
was lucky. The lady was very reluctant to pay her
stake this time, but the young man insisted. At last she
lifted a third plank, and out came the elder brother.
What a joy that was for both of them!

After the first happy embrace, both young men
turned upon the lady. She fell on her knees before
them. 'Don't kill me,' she said. 'I can be of service to
you. You are not out of danger, but I can save your
life.' Then she told them the secret of the fakir. He had

devoted his life to the service of Kali, the goddess of death. He believed that he could become perfect with the help of the spirits of dead men. Six times he had sacrificed men on the altar of Kali and had hung their heads in the temple. When he sacrificed the seventh, he would attain perfection; and the elder prince was to be that victim.

The two young men went at once to the temple. The elder brother entered, and ghostly laughter filled the building. It came from six skulls which hung in the roof. He asked why they laughed, and they all replied that they were pleased to see that he was going to join their company. They laughed again, most horribly, and the young man was afraid, but answered boldly: 'Is there no help for me, then?'

One of the skulls said: 'You could help yourself, and us too. When the fakir brings you to the temple, he will tell you to kneel before the goddess. Then as you bow he will cut off your head. But you must pretend that, being a prince, you have never been taught to bow down your head to others. Tell him that he must show you how it is done. Then, as he kneels, you must act quickly.' And all the skulls laughed again at the thought.

The two brothers went back to the fakir's hut and worked away quietly, as if nothing had happened. Then the day came when the fakir's period of meditation and prayer was ended. In the morning he told the elder prince that he must go to offer prayers at the temple. The young man said nothing, but the brother insisted on going too. When they reached the temple, only the elder was allowed inside. The fakir stood before the statue of the goddess, stayed a while in prayer, and said: 'Bow down low before the great goddess.'

The young man said proudly: 'You forget who I am. I am no slave to be always kneeling down and humbling myself. I am a prince of the royal blood. I have never bowed down to anyone. If you want me to—and I am willing to kneel to the goddess but to no man—you must show me how.'

'You waste time, boy,' said the fakir and impatiently pushed him aside. Then he went down on his knees and bowed his head low. The prince raised his sword, and took off the fakir's head at a single blow. All the skulls in the temple roof laughed aloud.

The brothers quickly cut down all the skulls and lay them in a row before the altar. Then the elder prince sprinkled the fakir's blood on them, and at once they were joined to their bodies and came back to life. Then they all laughed indeed!

The two princes returned home, and their life-trees grew green for many a long year.

Justice for Kangalu

One morning the Brahman's wife awoke with a great craving for fish. What wouldn't she give for a fine fat filleted steak? She badgered her husband until he, for peace and quiet, agreed to go to market and buy what he could. He had no money, but the neighbours were generous and, an anna here, a pice there, he managed to collect a couple of rupees. With this wealth he went off to the fish shop.

There he bought a magnificent fish. Then he went around the stalls buying vegetables to go with it. In the end he had a big heap of purchases, and he did not fancy carrying them all the way home. There were plenty of coolies standing around waiting to be hired, but none of them wanted such a heavy job. Besides, the Brahman had spent all his money, and even a coolie cannot live on promises.

At last a big strong man made a bargain with him. 'Holiness, I'll carry the food home if you agree to give me one good meal of the fish.' 'Right!' said the Brahman. 'Pick it up and we'll be on our way. What's your name?'

'Kangalu,' said the big man, and bent to his load.

When they got home, the wife was delighted. The fish was fatter even than she had expected. She made a great show of preparing the meal and made all the neighbours come and admire the fish. She served it with a mountain of rice and other good things. The Brahman sat down and ate heartily. Then his wife put away a large amount inside her until she could scarcely move. She just had strength enough to store away the remains of the feast, and then stumbled off to

bed where the Brahman was already snoring.

But what about Kangalu? He was not too happy seeing all that good food disappearing down other people's throats. However, he comforted himself with the thought that when the wife awoke she would give him the promised meal. But the two went on sleeping, and he became ever hungrier and more discontented.

At last the Brahman stirred. He called out drowsily: 'Kangalu, tell me a story.'

'Well I'll be damned!' said Kangalu to himself in great indignation. Then he said aloud in a sing-song voice: 'The deer goes on three legs. Who can catch his tail?'

'What's all that?' said the Brahman. 'What deer?'

'The one that has just run down the street,' said Kangalu.

The Brahman jumped out, grabbed a stick, and ran out of the house. Just then his wife awoke, and said: 'Kangalu, where has my husband gone?'

'Oh, he's just gone out for a minute,' said Kangalu. 'A pretty girl was going by and he went to speak to her. They went off that way, arm in arm.'

'The old devil!' screamed his wife. 'I'll teach him to carry on,' and she picked up her broom and ran off down the street.

Now they were both out of the way, Kangalu could give some thought to his empty belly. He hastily gathered together a good quantity of food, warmed it up in the pan, and then began eating as quickly as he could, using both hands. He was still at it when the Brahman and his wife came back. The Brahman was furious, for Kangalu, being of low caste, had contaminated all the food he had touched and it would all have to be thrown away. 'You scoundrel!' he shouted. 'You've ruined it all.'

'I only took what I had been promised,' said Kangalu humbly.

'Don't you give me that talk,' said the Brahman. 'You'll come along to court.'

'Very well,' said Kangalu; so the Brahman tied a rope around his wrist and led him away to justice.

On the way they passed a food shop. 'Holiness, I want to buy something,' said Kangalu.

'Oh, all right!' said the Brahman, and let go of the rope. Kangalu went in and asked the price of some baskets of rice.

'Eighty cowries,' said the shopkeeper.

'I've only got seventy-nine,' said Kangalu.

'That's no use,' said the shopman. 'I'd as soon let my rice go for eighty cowries and a slap in the face as sell at less than the right price.'

Kangalu nodded his head, went out and begged a cowrie from a passer-by, then went back into the shop. He handed the shopkeeper the eighty cowries, took a basket of rice, and then gave the poor man a mighty slap in the face. 'What do you think you are up to?' said the man, astonished. 'How dare you hit me?'

'I was only keeping my side of the bargain,' said Kangalu.

'I'll have you in court for this,' said the shopkeeper, and tied a rope to his other wrist. Off went Kangalu with the shopman on one rope and the Brahman on the other.

After a while Kangalu said: 'Holiness, I want to soak my rice in water.'

'Very well.' So they let go of the ropes, and Kangalu went to a house and spoke to the man who sat outside: 'Would your highness let me have the use of a plantain leaf?'

Now it happened that the man had just had a row

with his wife and had come outside to cool off. He was still very angry, so he said to Kangalu: 'Get inside and ask that daughter of a dung-eater!'

In went Kangalu and started to shout at the top of his voice: 'O daughter of a dung-eater! I want a plantain leaf.'

The husband came and grabbed him by the neck, saying angrily: 'How dare you talk to my wife like that!'

'I only did what you told me,' said Kangalu meekly. 'I thought that must be her name.'

'You'll answer for this in court,' said the husband, and tied a rope around Kangalu's leg. So off he went again with three men on the ropes.

After a time they came up with a man selling oil. 'How far is it to the palace?' asked Kangalu.

'A good way yet,' said the man. 'You won't get there before the court rises at the rate you are going. If you can liven up you may get there in time.'

'Oh, we've got a bit slack,' said Kangalu cheerfully. 'Perhaps this will liven things up,' and he gave the oil-man a great blow in the face. 'What the devil is that for?' shouted the man. 'I'll have the law on you.'

'Come on then,' said Kangalu, holding out his free foot, and the oil-man tied a rope to it.

When Kangalu and his four companions arrived at the palace, the court had already broken up. So they had to put up for the night. Next morning they marched into court and the Rajah's chief minister heard their case.

He listened carefully while the Brahman made his complaint about the fish. Then he said: 'Brahman, you are in the wrong. You did not fulfil your bargain, and Kangalu had the right to take what was due to him.'

Next the shopkeeper spoke. The Minister said: 'You are in the wrong. You invited Kangalu to slap you in the face, and he did so. You have no complaint.'

The husband next made his complaint about the insult to his wife. The Minister said: 'You too are in the wrong. Kangalu only followed your own bad example and you are to blame for that.'

Lastly the oil-man was called. He told his story. 'Kangalu,' said the Minister severely, 'you are to blame in this. You struck this man without any excuse. You will pay a fine of eight annas.'

Kangalu felt in his bag, but could find only a single rupee. He stepped forward, laid this coin on the Minister's table, then leaned forward and gave him a sharp slap on the cheek.

'You scoundrel!' shouted the Minister. 'How dare you strike me?'

'My Lord!' said Kangalu very humbly. 'The only money I had was a rupee, but my fine was eight annas. I couldn't get change here. So I gave you a slap. That made us square. One slap—a fine of eight annas. Two slaps—one rupee.'

The Minister was not amused, but the Rajah, who had been sitting in court, laughed heartily and announced that justice had been done.

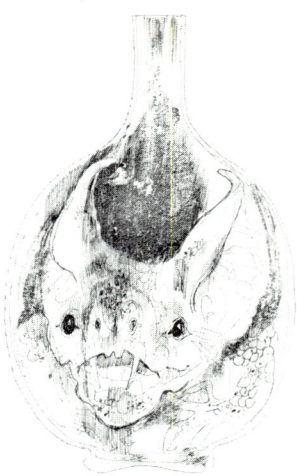

The Ghostly Double

There was a good young Brahman who wanted to get married. The trouble was that he was exceedingly poor. Not only would he find it difficult to keep a wife in food; he could not find the money to pay for the wedding and for presents to give to the bride's mother and father. But he did so want a wife.

When you want something badly enough you go to all sorts of extremes to get it. This Brahman took his bowl and went begging from door to door. He flattered all the wealthiest men in a shameless fashion. After a long time he found that he had just enough to meet the cost of the wedding.

So at last he brought home his pretty bride and showed her proudly to his mother, who of course still lived with him.

He was very happy for a time. Then he found that all his savings were gone and he was as poor as ever, and this time he could see no hope of finding any more money. He had used up his credit with his neighbours and the rich people now knew him too well to be taken in by his flattery.

At last he said to his mother: 'There's no help for it. I shall have to go away in search of my fortune. I don't know how long I shall be, but I will not come back until I have a large sum of money. You must manage as best you can while I am away, and take great care of my dear wife.'

So he went off. That was in the morning. In the evening, a figure which looked exactly like the Brahman appeared at the house. It was in fact his ghostly double. The wife was surprised and said: 'How is it you are home so soon? We were not expecting you for years. Have you changed your mind?'

The ghost said—and its voice was just like the Brahman's—'It was a bad day for travelling. Besides, I managed to get some money during the day.'

Wife and mother were sure that this was the Brahman. So the ghost settled down and lived in the house and went about his everyday affairs. The neighbours too had no doubt that this was indeed the Brahman. And so it went on for several years.

Then the real Brahman came home. Wasn't he surprised to find someone looking just like him living in his house? And he was not too pleased about it!

He said: 'What is all this about? Who are you living in my house?'

The ghost said: 'I don't know what you are talking about. This is my house, and my mother, and my wife. Be off with you!' And he chased the Brahman away with a stick.

Here was a puzzle for the poor Brahman. What was he to do? It seemed best to him to get support from the authorities, so he went off to see the king. The king heard the case in his court, and called both the Brahman and the ghost before him. He looked from one to the other, and they were as much alike as could be. It was quite beyond him to make a fair judgment, so he sent them both away. The Brahman went back next day, and the next, and the next, but still the king would not give his verdict. The unhappy Brahman beat his head and wept, saying: 'What a world this is! Here am I driven out of my own house and some stranger has stolen both house and wife. And what a king! He can't even make up his own mind.'

As he came away from the palace after yet another unsatisfactory day in court, he walked through a meadow where cows grazed. This was a favourite playground for the cowherds. They used to let the cows go where they wanted while they played their games. Their favourite pastime was Kings and Queens. One boy was chosen as king, while others took the parts of prime minister, chief of police, treasurer, and so on. As they played they noticed the Brahman, who was weeping bitterly. The boy-king ordered the man to be brought before him, and one of the boys ran over and said to the Brahman: 'The king commands you to come to him.'

'I've had enough of kings!' said the Brahman bitterly. 'He's no use to me. I've already seen him once today. What does he want with me now?'

'No, no,' said the boy. 'It isn't the real king. Our cowherd king wants you.'

'Who on earth is a cowherd king?' said the Brahman.

'Come and see.' So the Brahman decided to join in the game.

'Why do you come here weeping every day?' said the boy-king. The Brahman saw no harm in telling him the story, so that is what he did. The boy listened carefully. Then he said: 'I see. It seems to me that you are telling the truth. So this is what we will do; you must go back to the king and ask him to hand over the case to me for judgment.'

Back went the Brahman, and the king heard what he had to say. The real king was only too glad to be rid of this troublesome case, so he readily agreed. The trial was called for the following day.

The Brahman and his ghostly double attended in the cows' meadow. The cowherd king was there, sitting on an old wooden throne with a few rags draped around him instead of robes. He had brought with him a bottle with a narrow neck. The mock-king heard what both sides had to say and called a number of witnesses. When he thought it had gone on long enough, the boy-king said: 'That will do. We have heard enough evidence. Now we shall give judgment. Do you see this bottle? Whichever of you shall go inside it shall be judged the rightful owner of house and wife. Now, who will try first?'

The Brahman said: 'Who expects to hear sense from a cowherd? Silly boy, how could a man get into that little bottle?'

'Then you cannot be the rightful owner,' said the boy. 'Now you, sir,' turning to the ghost. 'If you go in, then the house and its contents must be yours.'

'Easily done,' said the ghost, and without another word he squeezed himself up as small as a beetle and crept into the neck of the bottle. The boy-king quickly put in the cork, and there was the ghost, safely caught.

The boy handed the bottle to the Brahman, and said: 'I advise you to throw this into the deepest bottom of the sea. Then go back to your house and your wife, and good fortune go with you.'

And that is what the Brahman did.

The Bald Wife

There was a merchant who had married two wives. He loved the younger one better than the other, because she was prettier, although, to tell the truth, they were neither the one nor the other what one could call beautiful. They were both short of hair, but while the younger had two tufts the older had only one.

The husband was away for much of the time going about his business, and so the wives were thrown into one another's company a great deal. This was a pity, because they did not get on well; in fact they heartily disliked one another. The younger made the most of being the husband's favourite. She made her companion do all the heavy work about the house, she nagged her all the time, and gave her just enough food to keep the life in her.

One day she said to the older wife: 'Come and comb my hair.' The elder was pulling the comb through one of the locks when it came out in her hands. Well, you may imagine how angry the younger wife was. She grabbed the older by her single lock of hair and tore it out of her head. Then she turned her out of the house.

The poor woman, now completely bald, was cast down with misery. She did not care what happened to her, so she wandered off into the jungle, expecting that she would end her life under the claws of some wild animal. On the way she passed a cotton plant that had been neglected. Making herself a broom of sticks she swept around the plant so that the rain could get to its roots. Then she went on and noticed a plantain tree. This too she tidied up. Next she came to the shed of a big white Brahmani bull. She took her broom to this too, much to the delight of the sacred animal, which bellowed its thanks.

Very soon she came to a hut made of trees and leaves, outside which a holy man sat cross-legged deep in meditation. She came up quietly behind him. 'Whoever you are,' he said, 'come out from behind me, or I shall turn you to ashes where you stand.'

She did not need to be told twice! She came and knelt at his feet, trembling in awe because she could feel his power. 'What do you want with me,' he said.

'Father,' said the wife. 'You know everything, so you must know of my unhappiness. My husband does not love me, and his other wife has driven me out, bald, to die in the wilderness. Will you take pity on me in my misery?'

He sat for a moment in thought. Then he said: 'You see that tank over there. Go and plunge just once in the water. Then come back to me.'

She went to the water and quickly dipped herself so that she was quite covered. Then she climbed out and stood dripping. What a change! Her head was now covered with thick hair, shining and black, and so long that it touched her heels. All her wrinkles had gone and her skin was smooth and rosy. She looked a young woman and a very beautiful one.

Overjoyed, she went and threw herself on the ground in front of the wise man and embraced his feet. 'Get up,' he said. 'Now go into the hut. You will find a number of baskets there. Choose whichever one you like and bring it out to me.'

She did as she was told. There were baskets of all sizes, some rich in jewels, some plain. She picked out one of the more humble baskets and took it to the man. 'Open it,' he said. She did so, and it was full of precious stones. 'It is yours,' he said. 'It will never

grow empty. When you take out a stone, another will come in its place. Now go in peace.'

With this blessing she went back rejoicing. On the way the Brahmani bull gave her two shells which were twined around its horns, and told her to wear them on her wrists. She did so, and shook her arms admiringly. Out of the shells fell fine ornaments of gold and silver. Then the plantain gave her one of its leaves, which would provide her always with rich foods. Lastly the cotton plant gave her one of its branches. 'Shake it,' said the plant. She obeyed, and a bolt of the finest silk dropped into her lap. She took off her shabby cotton saree and wrapped the silk round her hips so that she looked like a queen. Then she went home.

The younger wife, standing at the door, did not recognize the beautiful woman who stopped outside. When at last she realised who it was, she was quite overcome with wonder. What had happened to the old wrinkled, bald-headed crone whom she had chased away? Here was a marvel!

The beautiful wife could not have been kinder. She treated the other with great affection, and gave her fine clothes and ornaments, and denied her nothing that she wanted. She could have grown fat and happy. But no! The younger wife was filled with jealousy and evil thoughts. She too must be made beautiful.

She listened to the other wife's story of her adventures. Then she too set out for the jungle. But what a difference! She walked past the cotton plant, and the bull, and the plantain, with her head in the air, and did nothing for them. Then she came and stood boldly before the holy man. He told her to dip once in the water. She did, and came out as beautiful as could be. Dissatisfied, she decided to try again. In she plunged and came out as ugly as she had been before.

The wife went and grovelled before the holy man, weeping and pleading for mercy. 'Be off with you, you foolish woman,' he shouted and sent her howling on her way.

Soon after she got home, the husband returned from his travels. He at once fell deeply in love with his beautiful wife. Never had he imagined such loveliness. He could not do enough for her, especially when he found that she had endless supplies of clothes and food and ornaments. They lived together in great comfort and contentment, and the other wife stayed with them as their servant.

The Magic Ring

The merchant's son was now old enough to make his own way in the world. His father gave him three hundred rupees with which to start his fortune, gave him his blessing too, and sent him on his way.

The young man strode out boldly, but he had not gone far when he came upon a crowd of men quarrelling over a dog. Some of them said: 'He's a useless animal, not worth his food.' Others were against killing the beast. The young man was moved to pity by the dog and pleaded for his life.

'Let him go, and I'll pay you a hundred rupees,' he said, and they were only too glad to accept.

Off went the young man with only two hundred rupees now, but with a fine dog at his heels. Before long he met a crowd squabbling about a cat. 'She'll never catch another rat,' some said; 'She's past it, and we might as well drown her.' Others thought that this was unfair. Our kind lad of course sided with the cat.

'Let me have her,' he said. 'I'll give you a hundred rupees.' They did not think twice about this offer, and the young man continued on his way, his fortune down to a hundred rupees but a contented cat sitting on his shoulder, purring loudly.

At the next village there was a crowd in the square arguing about a snake which had just been caught. 'Nasty, poisonous thing!' said some. 'Break its back with a stick.' Others wanted to let it go. What did our young man do? Why, he offered his last hundred rupees in exchange for its life. The villagers were pleased to agree, and the snake gratefully coiled around the lad's waist.

What was he to do now? All his money was gone, together with his hopes for a prosperous future. All he could do was turn round and go back home.

'You stupid clown!' said his father. 'I didn't give you my hard-earned money to throw away on trash. Into the stables with you! You are not fit to live with humans.' And into the stables he had to go.

It could have been worse. He had plenty of straw to lie on, and his animals helped to keep him warm. The cat cuddled his feet, the dog acted as his pillow, and the snake lay across his body with its head hanging down on one side and its tail the other.

One day the snake said: 'My father is a king, Raja Indrasha. I wish you could meet him. I should very much like to tell him that you saved my life, so that he could reward you.'

'I should be honoured to meet His Highness,' said the young man politely. 'Where does he live?'

'Do you see that mountain?' said the snake. 'At its foot there is a sacred spring. If you will go there with me and dive into the water, we shall come up in my father's kingdom. He will be so pleased to see you. I know he will offer you any reward you like. When he does, you must ask for the ring from his right hand and his pot and spoon. Don't forget. Nothing else will do.'

So it was agreed, and on the right day the young man set out for the mountain with his three companions. When they got to the spring, the young man prepared for his dip. The cat and the dog said to him: 'What about us? What shall we do?'

'Just wait here. I shan't be long.' And then he and the snake plunged into the water and disappeared.

'Now what shall we do?' asked the dog.

'Just do what you are told,' said the cat. 'If you are

worried about your belly, as you usually are, I'll go into the town and beg for food. We shall have plenty to keep us fed until the master returns.' And so she did, and they settled down comfortably by the water.

What about the young man and his snake? They swam on through the water and at last came up in a strange country. When the king heard that his son had returned, he was overjoyed and at once sent orders that the snake should come to him. But the snake refused. 'I am in debt to a stranger,' he said. 'This man saved my life and, until the debt is paid, I must stay with him as his slave.' So the king welcomed the young man and kissed him, and offered him anything in the kingdom.

'Thank you, Highness,' said the lad. 'But I want only the ring from your right hand and your pot and spoon.' Although these were his greatest treasures, the king gave them to the young man without a word, and the lad bade the snake an affectionate farewell and went back. There were the cat and the dog, and a happy reunion it was for all three.

They walked together on the river bank for a while, and then the merchant's son decided to try out his new treasures. He turned the ring on his finger and said: 'I would like a nice house', and at once there was a magnificent house, richly furnished. Next he said: 'I should like to have the most beautiful princess in the world.' There she was, even more lovely than he had imagined. He spoke to the pot and the spoon and they produced a meal of the most delicious food, which he and the princess shared, and the animals had the scraps.

By now he was over his ears in love with the princess. It was not really suitable, for they were of different castes, but he just could not help himself. He asked her to marry him and she agreed. So they were married, and lived very agreeably in the fine house by the river, and the dog and the cat kept them company.

One morning the princess sat by the river combing her long golden hair. A few hairs came out, and she amused herself making a little boat out of reed, put the hair into it, and sent it sailing down the river. It floated on for many miles, into the neighbouring kingdom. A prince was sitting on the river-bank. He saw the boat and drew it to land, and, looking inside, he saw the golden hair. At once he fell desperately in love with the owner of the hair. He ran home, locked himself in his room, and refused either to leave it or to take food.

His father, the king, was very distressed. What was he to do with his son? He would not eat, or drink, or sleep, and would talk of nothing but the woman with the golden hair. If nothing were done, the young prince would surely die, and the kingdom would lose its heir.

In his trouble the king decided to consult an aunt of his. This was a dangerous course, for the old lady, besides being very wise, was an ogress and a mistress of all sorts of magic. However, she listened to the king's story and said that she would do what she could to help him.

She sniffed at the hair. Then she turned herself into a bee and flew along the river buzzing and buzzing and smelling with her sensitive nose. Soon she came to the princess's house. She turned herself back into an old woman, and went to the house leaning on a stick. When the princess came to the door the old woman announced herself as her aunt. 'You don't know me, my dear,' she said, 'because I have been living away ever since you were born. But I had to call on you just as soon as I got back.' And she kissed the princess fondly.

To tell the truth, the princess had been rather lonely and homesick and she was glad to find a new friend. She gave the old woman a warm welcome and invited her to stay just as long as she liked. The woman thought to herself that all had gone better than she could have hoped. She let three days go by while she got herself settled into the house and into the princess's confidence. Then she coaxed her to talk about the magic ring. 'It can't be very safe in your husband's care,' she said. 'He is always going off on these hunting trips of his, and he could easily lose it. If I were you, I would get him to let you look after it.'

This seemed a sensible suggestion, and the princess took it up. Her husband agreed immediately, and so the princess put the ring on her own finger.

The ogress waited another day, and then she asked the princess to show her the wonderful ring. The princess slipped it off her finger. Directly the old woman had her hands on it, she turned herself back into a bee and flew home at top speed. There lay the prince, very close to death. 'Cheer up, lad!' said the ogress. 'I have something here that will get you your heart's desire.' Then she showed him the ring and explained how it worked. Immediately he ordered the ring to bring him the princess and her house, and it obeyed him. The house appeared in the grounds outside the prince's palace. The prince jumped out of bed, quite cured of his sickness, and rushed in search of his love. She was upset by the loss of her precious ring and of her new-found aunt, not to mention the flight of her house, and she was in no state to listen to his words of love. When she came to her senses, she realised that this handsome young prince was asking her to marry him. What could she do? She had no idea where she was, or how to get back to her husband. 'Very well,' she said, when the prince paused for breath. 'I will marry you, but you must wait one month for me.'

'I will wait a thousand years,' he said, 'but don't keep me a minute longer than you must.'

What about the princess's husband? He came back from his hunting to find that this wife and his house had both vanished. You may imagine what a state he was in. He sat down in despair and made up his mind to put an end to his miserable life. At this point the cat and the dog appeared. They had gone into hiding when the house shot up into the air, but now they ventured out. 'Cheer up, master!' said the cat. 'Things are difficult but they might be worse. Just give us a month, and we will do our best to recover your princess and your house.'

'Do that,' he said, 'and I shall agree to go on living.'

The cat and the dog hurried off and did not stop for breath until they found where their mistress had been taken. 'This will not be easy,' said the cat. 'You stay here, and I will try to find the princess.' So the cat leapt up to a window-ledge and looked in. There sat the beautiful princess, weeping. She knew the cat at once and let her in, telling her of the plight she found herself in.

'What shall I do?' she said in despair.

'The first thing,' said the cat, 'is to get hold of the ring. Where is it now?'

'In the ogress's belly,' wept the princess. 'She has swallowed it.'

'Don't worry,' said the cat. 'I'll get it.'

Then the cat went and lay down by a rat hole, pretending to be dead. She knew that a big wedding was taking place in the rat community that day. All the rats in the kingdom would be coming this way, for the rat prince himself, heir to the kingdom, was to be the bridegroom. Very soon a procession appeared, and in the middle was the rat prince himself in all his wedding finery. As he came to the hole the cat sprang suddenly to life. She caught the bridegroom in her paws and sat on him.

'Mercy! mercy!' screamed the rat. 'Let me go!'

'Yes, let him go! It's his wedding day,' squeaked all the other rats.

'Listen,' growled the cat. 'I'll make a bargain with you. The ogress who lives in this house has stolen a ring belonging to my master. She has swallowed it for safe keeping. If you get it back for me, I'll let this little creature under my paws go free. If not, you must start looking for another prince to rule you.'

'We will do it,' said the rats. 'If we fail, you can eat the lot of us.'

The rats waited until it was night and the ogress was asleep. Then they went into her bedroom. There she lay, on her back with her mouth open, snoring. One of the rats climbed on to her face and dangled his tail in her mouth. She gulped and spluttered, and up came the ring. Another rat was on to it in a flash and ran off with it in his mouth. The cat took the ring and graciously let go of the prince, who went off, much shaken, to continue his wedding ceremony.

The cat and the dog set off for home. They were in high spirits and looked forward to their master's pleasure at getting his ring back. They made good progress, but were checked by a stream across their path. The cat climbed on to the dog's back and the dog swam. But the dog was jealous because the cat had the ring. Halfway across he stopped swimming and

threatened to throw the cat into the water if she did not give him the ring. What could the cat do? She gave it up, very reluctantly, and the clumsy dog dropped it into the water. Up swam a fat fish and swallowed it.

'Oh, oh! What shall I do?' yelped the dog.

'What's done is done,' said the cat. 'We shall just have to get it back. I have an idea. You go and kill a young lamb.'

The dog did as he was told. He caught a lamb, killed it, and tore out its insides. Then the cat put on the lamb's skin and lay down quite still by the stream. Very soon, up flew a fish-eagle and pounced on the lamb. What a surprise the bird got when the cat jumped out and grabbed him! The cat ordered the eagle to catch the fish, which it did, and so the cat got back her ring.

'Come on, we have wasted enough time,' said the cat.

'No, I won't,' barked the dog. 'I'm going to carry the ring. You get all the praise, and I get nothing but blame. Give me the ring, or I'll bite you in two.'

The cat did not like it at all, but she gave up the ring. They had not gone a mile before the dog had dropped it again. A kite saw it sparkle and flew down, took the ring in its beak and flew into a high tree.

'Dear, oh dear!' said the dog. 'I've done it again.'

'Keep quiet, or you will frighten the bird right away.'

They waited until it was getting dark. Then the cat climbed the tree unseen, and killed the bird before it knew what was happening. She recovered the ring and climbed to the ground.

'Come along, do!' she said. 'Our master has suffered enough.'

This time the dog did not argue. He was thoroughly ashamed of his folly and clumsiness. So they finished their journey quickly and gave their master the ring. Believe me, he wasted no time. He gave the ring its instructions, and at once his house returned. Inside was his lovely wife, and wasn't she glad to see him? They settled down to enjoy their happiness, and they did not forget the cat, or even the foolish dog, with whom they shared their joy for many years.

Kanai the Gardener

Whatever else you might say about him, Kanai was a good gardener. He really gave himself to his work, body and soul.

He worked for the king in a garden which was as good as you might find in all India. It had all kinds of flowering plants and trees as well as fruits, and there was a beautiful water-garden. Kanai was there from morn to night.

In fact one night he was still there after dark. There was a full moon and he could see well enough as he made his final round of the garden. Then, all at once he heard a tremendous noise. All the plants bent as if under a strong wind and some of the trees snapped off at ground level. Kanai was in a fine panic. He hid behind the trunk of a very big tree and waited to see what would happen. Soon he saw a great elephant coming down out of the sky, and the animal landed in the garden and wandered off out of sight.

After a while Kanai came out from his hiding-place and sat on the water's edge. He thought to himself: this must surely be Airavata, the god Indra's own elephant, come down from heaven. I had better see what it is up to.

So he followed the beast's great footsteps and watched as it ate the fruit and tore up trees by the roots. At last it prepared to fly home, and as it rose from the ground Kanai grabbed it by the tail and went up to heaven.

In heaven the elephant went off to Indra's palace, and Kanai set about exploring. He was amazed at what he saw. There were the same kinds of things in heaven

as on earth, but they were so much bigger and finer, and so cheap too. He had a few coins in his pocket, so he wandered through the bazaar, buying some tasty sweets and eating them as he went. Then he bought some pan-leaf and a betel-nut, both bigger than he would have thought possible. He kept these to take home. Then he sat down to wait until Airavata paid his next visit to earth. As night was falling the elephant flew off with Kanai dangling from his tail.

When they landed, Kanai hurried off home. His wife ran to meet him, crying: 'Where have you been? I have been so worried.' Instead of explaining, Kanai just got out the bargain he had bought in heaven. His wife was delighted with the great betel-nut. 'Wherever did you get it?' she gasped, and then he told her his amazing story.

She said at once: 'I'm coming too.'

'So you shall,' he said, 'but don't say a word to anyone else about it.'

'Not me,' said his wife. 'I'll not tell a soul.'

But when she went, later in the day, to draw water at the well, she met her best friend, so she told her the story as a very great secret. The friend told her neighbour, in confidence, and very soon everyone in the village had heard about Kanai's trip to heaven.

When evening came, twenty or more people went to the garden, all eager to buy bargains in the heavenly bazaar. Kanai was not too pleased. However there was nothing he could do about it, so he made them line up and then gave them their orders. 'I will hold the elephant's tail. My wife will hold me around the waist, and her friend will hold her. You will come next, and you there, and so on to the end of the line. Is that understood?'

They were all happy with this arrangement. Soon,

down crashed the elephant and went blundering through the garden. When it had finished eating, Kanai gripped its tail firmly, and his wife put her arms round him. All the other villagers formed a chain, and the elephant flew up into the sky with a long human tail trailing behind. They were several miles high, with all the world spread out below them, when Kanai's wife's best friend said to her: 'How big did you say that betel-nut was?'

'I'll ask my husband,' she said, and repeated the question to Kanai.

'I'll tell you when we get to heaven,' he said.

'No, no! I want to know now.'

'Can't it wait?'

'No. I must know now, this minute.'

'Oh, about so big,' said Kanai, and showed the size with his outstretched hands. In doing this he let go of the elephant's tail, and Kanai, his wife, her friends and neighbours, shot down to earth like so many shooting stars.

Two Wives and Two Brides

The Zemindar was the chief man of his village. He had wealth and a great reputation among his neighbours for wisdom and fair dealing. But he had no heir to carry on his name. As a young man he had married a wife, and when she had no children he married another, but still without success. His second wife turned out to be a gentle and kind woman, but the first was a terror, always ill-tempered and quarrelsome and one who heartily disliked her husband. Although he much preferred the younger wife, he showed his wisdom in being equally kind to both, and managed in this way to keep peace in his household. But it was not easy.

One day a beggar came to the door, asking for alms. The younger wife greeted him and ran at once to gather a generous helping of scraps from the kitchen. He thanked her and said: 'My blessing on you and your children.'

'I have no children,' she replied.

'Then I cannot take your gift,' he said. 'A childless woman brings misfortune, and the food you have touched will be tainted.' And with that he went off to try his luck at another house.

She was dreadfully upset. Her husband found her crying her heart out, saying 'I can't bear it and I can't bear it!' When he asked what was the matter, she told him the whole story, declaring that she would not go on living.

'Don't weep,' he said gently. 'There's no point in grieving about something which is not your fault. If

God says that you are not to have a child, who are we to complain? Still, I will see if anything can be done.'

A few days later the same beggar returned and sought out the Zemindar. He said: 'I hear that your wives have not been blessed with children. I know that you are a good man and deserve an heir, so I have made up a drug which will help. Give it to your wife and you shall have an heir.'

The elder wife had been listening at the door. When the beggar had gone, she came out, snatched the bottle, and said: 'I'll have that!'

Her husband said: 'It is not for you alone, but for both of my wives. See that you share it with your companion.'

'Very well!' she said, and went away. She poured the drug into a mortar and gave it a good pounding with the pestle until it was thoroughly ground. Then she ate the lot.

Soon, the younger wife came to her and said: 'I hear that the beggar has brought us a drug which will make us pregnant. Give me my share.'

'I'm sorry, my dear,' said the other. 'There was so little of the drug that there was only enough for one. Never mind; I'll let you nurse my baby from time to time.'

Well, you can imagine how the younger wife felt. She went away and wept in her room. Then she had an idea. She found the mortar in which the drug had been mixed, and washed it and the pestle very carefully. Then she drank the water.

In a short time both wives found that they were pregnant. Wasn't the Zemindar pleased? He made a great fuss of both wives, and spent a vast amount of money in preparations for the births. And in time both wives had baby daughters. The younger wife's child was a pretty one, but the elder's was as ugly as you'd find in a day's march! The Zemindar put a good face on his fortune, but he found it difficult not to show how ugly he found his elder daughter, while he couldn't get enough of the younger one's company. He was always nursing her and kissing her.

Of course the elder wife knew what he thought, and she sometimes very nearly burst with jealousy. She searched her wicked mind to find how she could make away with the pretty child.

Time passed, and the children grew up. The younger was even lovelier now, and the other more hideous. She was nasty too, always spiteful and greedy, while her sister grew ever kinder and more gentle.

Tilbhushki—that was the younger girl—had plenty of suitors. The sister—Chalbhushki—had none, and never seemed likely to have any. Everyone hated her, and if she came into sight the neighbours used to grab their brooms and chase her off, shouting 'Away with you, and don't come back!'

Then, one day, the prince of that country went hunting. After a long day's sport he found that he had lost his companions and was all alone in the forest. He was tired and hungry and had no idea at all where he was. All he could do was ride ahead and see where he got to. So, on a horse as tired as he was, he came in the last light of day to the Zemindar's village. He went to the biggest house, which was of course the Zemindar's own, and out came the master to welcome him. He sat down to a fine meal and was then glad to sleep.

In the morning he looked out and saw a most beautiful girl. Never had he seen a lovelier one! After the first wonderful shock he began to think seriously. Surely this girl was fit to be a princess! He said to his host: 'Who is that girl?'

'My daughter.'

'Is she married?'

'Not yet.'

'Then', said the prince, 'will you consider me as a suitor? My father is the king. I know that you are a Brahman and of higher caste than me, but you will not find me unworthy of your daughter.'

'It would be an honour for my girl to marry you,' said the Zemindar, and so it was arranged.

Why delay? They were married right away, in the village, and the Zemindar conducted the ceremony. There was great feasting, and everyone was joyful, none more than the prince and Tilbhushki. Everyone? No; the elder wife was furious and so was Chalbhushki. The wife went to her husband and said: 'You have insulted me and my child in marrying off your younger daughter first. I will no longer live with you.'

To tell the truth he was not sorry to see her go. She found herself a house a little way outside the village, and there she settled with her ugly daughter.

The prince and his bride went home after the celebrations, and the king and queen made much of their new daughter-in-law. But after a while she began to long to see her father again, so she went on a visit to him. On the way back she passed the house where her stepmother was living. The woman ran out, saying: 'Come along in. I must have a look at you.' And she began to admire her fine clothes and ornaments. She touched the earrings and the jewelled comb in the girl's hair, and as she fondled her head the old woman entangled a root in her locks. At once the girl was turned into a bird, which flew out of the house and away into the trees.

Tilbhushki's fine dress and jewels were left lying on the floor. The woman picked them up, called her ugly daughter, and at once dressed her in her sister's finery. Then she called the bearers who were waiting outside, the daughter climbed into the palki, and was carried off to the royal palace.

It was late when they got there and already dark. Chalbhushki went straight to the prince's room. In the dim light he did not recognize her. Pleased to see his young wife back from her journey, he embraced her lovingly. Then he sat down with the girl on his knee with his arms around her.

Now the bird which had been Tilbhushki had followed the palki and now sat on a branch just outside the window, where she could see everything that was happening inside. She sang loudly:

> He can't see who is on his knee;
> What a fool this prince must be!

The prince heard the song and looked out of the window. The sight of the bird made him feel very strange. The feeling that he had had for some time that all was not well became stronger. In the dark he peered at the woman beside him. He could not see her very well, but even in this light he could see that she was far from beautiful; in fact, rarely had he come across anyone as ugly as this.

The prince never said a word. He put the girl on her feet, and went out of the palace. There was the bird clear against the night sky. But as he went near it hopped away from branch to branch, all the time keeping out of reach, and always singing its little song. Then it flew away.

The prince was distracted. He blundered deeper into the forest, and became deeply disturbed as he realised that he had lost the bird. When his servants

came looking for him, they found him quite out of his wits, his fine clothes torn to rags, and singing in his crazy voice:

He can't see who is on his knee;
What a fool this prince must be!

Of course the king and queen were greatly distressed. They sent for the best doctors in the country, but no one could find the cause of the prince's sickness. The prince seemed to be fading away.

One day a bird-catcher came to the palace. He had for sale a rare bird which could talk in human speech. The king admired the bird and offered a hundred gold pieces, which the man gladly accepted. The king thought that so unusual an animal might amuse his son, so he had it taken to the prince's room. The prince seemed attracted to the bird, but still all he could do was weep continuously.

The bird fluttered at the end of its perch, then it slipped its foot out of the chain that held it, and flew to the prince's shoulder. From there it hopped to his lap and nestled there, as if lovingly. The prince began to stroke the bird, his fingers gently exploring its soft plumage. He found something hard caught in the feathers. Without thinking he pulled hard, and out came the root that Chalbhushki's mother had stuck into Tilbhushki's hair. Suddenly his bride was there with him, naked—for her sister still had her clothes— and beautiful. It needed only this to restore the prince to health.

When the full story had been told, Chalbhushki and her mother were banished to a distant corner of the country where they could do no more harm. Then the prince and his bride were free to be happy. Very soon the king made over his kingdom to them, and they lived and ruled well for many years.

Four Friends Learn the Secret of Life

The prince had three friends and they did everything together. Their fathers were the principal men in the kingdom: the prime minister, the chief of police and the richest merchant, and of course the prince's father was the king.

One day the four friends decided to go travelling in foreign parts. Early in the morning they set out on their horses, and they rode all day. Towards evening, when they had begun to look out for a place to spend the night, they came upon a temple alone in the forest. They peeped inside, and saw that a holy man was sitting there, so deep in meditation that he never noticed the travellers.

The friends settled down in the shelter of the temple wall. They were worried about danger from the wild animals which roamed in the forest, so they decided to divide the hours of darkness into four watches. Each man would sleep for three and keep watch for one.

They drew straws for the first watch, and the job fell to the merchant's son. The others lay down and were soon asleep. The young man walked up and down to keep awake, and from time to time he looked into the temple. It was near the end of his watch when he saw the hermit move for the first time, pick up a bone and speak some words very clearly over it. At once there was a strange clattering sound. From all sides bones appeared, moving steadily towards the temple. The hermit put his bone on the ground, and all the others lay down beside it making a big heap.

The merchant's son realised that his watch was over. He went and shook the police chief's son awake and lay down in his place without a word.

The second watcher also marched up and down and looked into the temple. There sat the silent hermit with a great heap of bones at his feet. The night was full of the noise of animals, hyenas and tigers, but none were to be seen. The hours went by. Then the watcher saw the hermit raise his hands over the bones and speak some words over them very clearly. At once the heap began to stir. The bones came clashing together and formed a skeleton.

But now it was time for the watch to change. The police chief's son awakened the prime minister's son, then lay down without a word and was soon asleep.

It was now deep in the night. Even the hunting beasts had gone back to their dens and only the ghosts were roaming abroad. The young man glanced into the temple and saw the silent hermit, and saw too what looked like a big skeleton lying in front of him. He marched up and down and tried to keep his spirits high, but it was cold and the darkness frightened him. He was glad when he saw that his watch was nearly over. He walked once more right around the temple and looked inside. The hermit stirred and lifted his hands on high. Then he spoke some words very clearly. At once muscle and flesh began to appear on the bones, then skin formed on every part. It was a strange and terrifying sight, and the watcher was not sorry to end his term of duty. He returned to the camp and shook the prince, who got up sleepily. Then the prime minister's son lay down and slept.

The prince was soon wide awake. He could feel even in the darkness that dawn was not far away, so he walked up and down cheerfully enough. In the temple he saw the hermit sitting with what looked like a lifeless animal of some kind in front of him. Gradually trees began to emerge from the black night and the roof of the temple stood out against the sky. A faint pink glow appeared in the east. As the first shaft of sunlight glowed red there was a sound inside the temple. The prince looked in and saw the hermit lift his hands over the animal. He spoke aloud very clearly a few words, and the creature sprang to its feet and rushed out of the temple.

Light came quickly now, and the prince roused his companions. They gathered their horses, mounted and rode on their way. Still they said nothing about the events of the night. But at midday they stopped to rest by a forest pool. As they lay there the prince said: 'Did you see anything unusual last night?' The friends were glad of the opportunity to talk about their strange experiences, and soon the whole story had been told. 'It looked to me like a deer,' said the prince; 'the thing that ran off into the forest.'

They still marvelled over what they had seen. 'Do you realise what has happened?' said the prince. 'We may have learnt the secret of life. Do you all remember what words the hermit used?' The friends could all remember them distinctly, so they decided to put their knowledge to the test. They cast about in the forest and found a small bone. The merchant's son recited his words, and soon there was a big heap of bones in front of them. The police chief's son spoke his words over them, and they joined together to make the skeleton of some large beast. Now it was the prime minister's son's turn. When he said his charm flesh and skin covered the bones, and there in front of them lay an enormous tiger. Even lifeless it terrified the friends. They all said: 'Don't say your charm, prince, or surely we shall all be eaten up.'

The prince was not so sure. 'We must know whether all the charms work equally well', he said, 'otherwise we shall always be left in doubt. We need not risk our lives. Here is a tall tree. Climb up high enough to be out of the tiger's reach, and I'll follow you just as soon as I have recited my words.'

The young men were not happy with this idea, but the prince could not be shifted. He must finish his experiment. So the friends climbed up high and looked down on the huge animal and the tiny prince. They saw him raise his arms and heard the magic words. Then he ran for his life and scrambled up beside them. The tiger came suddenly to life, gave a loud roar and sprang on the horses. It killed them with four sharp blows, then dragged one off into the jungle to eat at leisure.

The friends waited a long time, until the noise of the tiger's progress faded away. Then they climbed down nervously. Here was a problem. They had lost their means of transport and had to walk, and that was something they were not used to doing. However, they limped on for an hour or two until they came to the seashore. There they waited until a ship came into sight. They waved and shouted, and a small boat came and picked them up. The captain promised to set them down at the first port of call.

They sailed on for four or five days. There was no port in sight, but they caught a glimpse of towers in the distance and persuaded the captain to set them down not far away. So they walked until they came to a city. There were streets of shops, but not a single person in sight. Doors and windows stood open, yet every house was empty. Not even a horse or a cow, a hen or a rat stirred. It was like a city of the dead— except that there were no bodies. It was a strange and frightening place.

They walked through the silent streets and came to a great gatehouse. The gates were open and, although there were plenty of weapons about, no guards prevented them from walking through into the palace. It was a huge building with six big courtyards, all of them silent and empty. Then, as they entered a seventh court, they saw a movement and a flash of colour, and there stood four young women, each more beautiful than the last. The girls ran forward and each grabbed one of the friends by the arm, greeting them as if they were old friends and embracing them joyfully. They led the men into the palace where a great feast was laid out. The girls chattered happily but would not answer any questions about the mystery of the dead city.

After they had eaten their fill, each of the women led her companion away to a private room. The prince went with the youngest and most lovely of the four girls. When they were alone, she began to weep bitterly. He was surprised and puzzled, and asked what her trouble was. 'Oh, poor young prince!' she said. 'I grieve for you, and for myself, because we are both in the greatest danger. I am the princess of this city, but these three with me, who seem like lovely young girls, are really Rakshasis. They are monsters who descended on the city and killed and ate my parents and all my family. Then they ate the court and the king's ministers, then all the servants and everyone else in the city, even to the last animal. That is why the city is deserted. Everyone has gone to relieving the hunger of those three ogres. So far they have spared me, but only until it suits them to do away with me. But you and your friends are doomed to be eaten. That is why they welcomed you so warmly.'

The prince was horrified at what he had heard. 'But how do I know you are telling the truth?' he said. 'If they are Rakshasis, may not you be one too? You look just like them.'

'Watch closely, and you will see that our ways are quite different. As you well know Rakshasis are always hungry. The meals that ordinary mortals eat go no way towards satisfying them. Your friends will find that their women slip away at night and spend the hours of darkness ranging over the countryside in search of food. Tell them to keep watch and they will soon have the proof of what I have told you. Meanwhile I will keep you company all night long, because I am a woman and no demon.'

As soon as he could get them alone, the prince called together his three friends and told them what he had learnt. So they kept watch that night, and sure enough the three beautiful women slipped away in the depth of the night, when they thought the men were fast asleep, and did not return till dawn. They were so tired that they then slept through the day.

It seemed that the prince's woman was telling the truth, and that these were truly Rakshasis. The friends were surely in great danger, for when the beautiful demons grew tired of hunting at night they would take the food nearest to hand and that was the men. So the friends made their plans to escape while their women were sleeping. With the princess they patrolled the seashore watching for a passing ship. The princess had her jewels and other treasures always with her so that they could pay their passage.

One day they saw a ship far out to sea. They quickly made a signal, and a boat was lowered and rowed to land. They immediately struck a bargain with the captain and were rowed out to the ship, the princess urging on the oarsmen. Suddenly there was a dreadful yell from the shore. The Rakshasis had appeared! They had taken off their women's disguise, and now they were hideous giants. Far out as the ship was, it was still almost within reach of the monsters, and the friends shook as they saw the open jaws and the sharp

teeth eager to eat them.

They had gone just far enough to be safe. As the ship pulled farther out to sea, the Rakshasis screamed: 'Greedy sister! So you want to eat them all yourself, do you?' Then the ugly creatures went back to land, leaving the friends to think what those last words meant. Three of them had little doubt that they had got rid of three Rakshasis but were still at the mercy of the fourth. Only the prince knew very well that his princess was no ogress but a gentle and lovely woman.

The ship sailed on for a day and a night, then towards the end of the second day it came in sight of a port. There the four friends and the princess were put on land.

They travelled on for a time on foot. The princess, who had lived the sheltered life of the palace, soon became very tired and her tender feet were bruised on the rough road. She had to rest. The prince sent the merchant's son ahead to the nearest town in order to buy food. He was a long time, and the prince became impatient and sent the police chief's son after him. Soon the prime minister's son followed them. Still none of them came back, and at last the prince went off himself to find out what had happened.

The truth was that the three young men were afraid of the princess, believing her to be a Rakshasi. They deliberately abandoned her, and, when the prince turned up, they forced him to stay with them.

So there was the lovely princess all alone in the desert. When she had rested she decided to travel on alone, so she walked into the city and found a house where she could stay. Here she made enquiries and found out where the four friends were lodging. She guessed why she had been left alone and she made up her mind to teach the young men a lesson.

She sold some of her jewels, and took a big house in the best part of the city. Then she announced that she was setting up a games-house and that she would challenge all comers to play her at dice. Whoever beat her would receive a lakh of rupees, but if she won she would have the prize from the loser.

The friends heard the challenge, but did not know that it was the princess, for she had disguised herself and chosen a false name. The prince was too sad at losing his princess to want to play, but the other three friends thought they were the best dice players in the world and they eagerly took up the challenge. One by one they sat down with the mysterious woman, but she was too good for them. Soon all their money was gone, but still they played on. Deep in debt they were arrested by her servants and locked up in the cellars of her house until they could pay.

The prince heard what had happened, and he decided that he must do what he could to win back his friends' money. He came to the house and sat down with the princess, but he did not know her. They played, and at first she let him win. He became excited with success and raised his stakes. Then he began to lose, and before long he was deeper in debt than his friends. In came the servants and seized him and bound him with many ropes. They were dragging him down to the cellars when she decided that the joke had gone on long enough. She threw off her disguise and they were in each other's arms. The three friends were let out of prison and came, blinking and confused, before the princess. They were bitterly ashamed of what they had done, but she quickly forgave them and they were all happy.

It was now time for the friends to go home, and the king and queen gave them a royal welcome. The prince and the princess were married and there were great feasts and rejoicing.

Still the princess was not quite happy. Her parents and friends had all been killed by the Rakshasis. They had never been buried and their bones lay among the hills around their city. She had heard how the prince and his friends had learnt the secret of life, but the dead could not be restored to life while the Rakshasis were still free. So the prince and his friends repeated their journey to the temple in the forest. There sat the hermit, just as he had done before. They knelt before him and told him their story. When he heard that they needed the secret of death he sighed deeply, and then arose and went to the door of the temple. A deer was running past. The hermit took water and spoke some words very clearly over it. Then he sprinkled the water over the deer and it fell into dust. He spoke other words and the deer jumped up and ran away.

The friends then made their way back to the Rakshasis' city. As they approached the gate, out came the monsters, screaming and with open jaws. The prince spoke the words of death and scattered water over them, and suddenly there was nothing there but a pile of dust.

Then the four friends spoke the four spells of life, and the bones lying about the city came together, formed skeletons, were covered in flesh and skin, and finally came to life. King, queen, chief minister, chief of the household, cook, nurse, blacksmith and groom—the whole court, city and country were restored.

Imagine the princess's joy at seeing her parents and friends all singing and feasting and all sorrow forgotten. Now she could settle down to enjoy her life with her prince and his three faithful friends.

How the Sons got their Reward

The old man felt sure that death was coming for him. So he called his sons around him, and a great fuss they made, weeping and crying and tearing their hair. He blessed them and, more to their liking, shared among them all his great wealth.

So that was that. But—do you know?—he didn't die. The poor fellow got over his illness and seemed good for many more years. Were his sons pleased? They were not. They had got their hands on his money and were not going to let go. Meanwhile the old father had to go on living with his sons, and their wives—and these were far worse—grudging him every mouthful at dinner-time and even a corner of the house in which to sit. All through the long days he got not one kind word or helping hand from any of them.

No wonder he wished that death had kept his appointment on time. However, he bore his misery with great patience and by neither word nor expression showed how sadly he was disappointed in his children. Only to a friend did he open his mind, telling him all that he had to suffer. The friend was sorry to hear his tale and promised to see what he could do to help. He went away and thought hard. Then he had an idea. He called at the house again and had a long talk with his old neighbour. They agreed on a plan, and the poor old man learnt how to smile again just a little.

In the next few days there was quite a little procession of visitors to the old man. Each of the callers brought with him a heavy bag, and the old man stowed these gifts away under his bed. The sons were very curious, but their father would say nothing to them. However he talked to the neighbours, and a rumour got around that some of his friends had paid their debts and that he was now sleeping on a fortune in gold and coins.

Well, that made the sons change their tune. They couldn't do enough for the old man. The wives cooked him tasty dishes, and the sons were only too pleased to carry his chair to a warm corner. So it went on for two or three years, and contented years they were for the father. Then death paid another visit, and this time there was no mistake. The old man died, quietly and with no pain.

The sons carried him away to the burning ghats, with great weeping. Then they rushed back home, rummaged under the bed, and got out the heavy sacks. They cut the strings and tipped them up, and out fell heaps of stones and gravel.

And up in heaven the old man was smiling.

The Princess who Turned Night into Day

The Raja's son was mad on hunting. Every day he was away in the forest with his bow in search of wild animals, the bigger the better. Although his mother worried, she could do nothing to stop him, but she told him firmly: 'You may hunt to the north, and to the east, and to the south, but to the west you must never go.' And the prince said that he would obey her.

So he did for many days. Then it came to him one morning that he always hunted in the same places, and he was tired of chasing the same animals and they were tired of him too. He must try his luck in the west. So he entered the forbidden country, and it was much like the rest and even poorer in animals. All he could find was a flock of parrots, and they shot up into the air out of range, all but one bird, the biggest of all who was king of the parrots, and his name was Hiraman.

Hiraman saw that he had been left behind at the mercy of the young prince. He called out to the others: 'Hey, don't leave me, or I'll tell Princess Labam!' Scared at this threat, the parrots all returned to their king.

The prince was surprised that the parrot could talk and that the rest of the birds obeyed him. He said: 'Who is this Princess Labam? And where does she live?' But the parrots would not tell him. 'You'll never get there', was all that they would say.

The prince was angry at this. He threw down his bow in a rage and went home, sulking. When he got to the palace, he would say nothing to his parents. He refused to eat anything, but put himself to bed and stayed there for the best part of a week. The Raja was puzzled, and so was the Rani. He did not seem ill, and yet he would neither eat nor speak.

Then one morning he said to them: 'I must go and find her.'

'Who?' they said.

'The Princess Labam, of course. Do you know where she lives?'

Now it was for fear of Princess Labam that his mother had forbidden him to go into the western forest. She said: 'Alas, poor son! We don't know where she lives. All we know is that it is bad luck to find her or even to think about her. No good will come of your quest.'

The young man would not listen. 'I must find her if it kills me. If God wills I shall return to you, but go I must.'

So his parents had to let him have his way. His father gave him a fine horse and dressed him in rich clothes. He took his bow and other weapons, thinking that he might need them if he fell into danger. He also took a purse of gold. When he was ready and mounted, his mother pulled out her handkerchief and filled it with sweets and gave it to him. 'You may be hungry on the way,' she said.

So he set out, and rode through the day. Towards evening he came to a clearing in the jungle where there was a pool surrounded by trees. Here he bathed and watered his horse, and lay down to rest. 'I am hungry,' he said to himself. 'I'll try one of mother's sweets.' He took one out, but it had an ant in it. He tried another, and it was the same. So he spread them out on the ground, and sure enough there was an ant in each one. 'It can't be helped,' he said. 'As the ants have started them, they may as well finish them up.'

One of the ants, larger than the others, came over to him. It was the ant king. It said: 'You have been good to us, and we will be good to you. Call when you need our help.'

The prince could not see what help an ant could be, but he thanked the animal courteously. Then, after sleeping, he set out on his journey again. In another part of the forest he heard a loud roaring, and there lay a great tiger, lashing his tail with pain and fury because it had a thorn driven deep into its paw.

The young prince dismounted and came cautiously up to the beast. 'I will gladly help you,' he said; 'but if I do, will you repay me by gobbling me up?'

'Never!' said the tiger. 'Cure me of this pain, and I will be your friend always.' So the prince took out his knife, and ever so gently cut into the tiger's paw and took out the thorn. But careful as he was he could not help hurting the beast even more, and its howl echoed through the jungle. The tiger's mate heard the cry, and she came charging through the trees, ready to save her husband or avenge his death. 'Who hurt you, my darling?' she cried. 'Show me him, and I will kill him, man or beast.'

'Let him be,' said the tiger. 'It is a Raja's son who has taken a thorn out of my foot. Let him alone.'

Then the prince stood up, and the tiger and its mate made much of him, rubbing their great faces against him and purring loudly. Then they led him to their den and shared their dinner with him. He liked this so well that he stayed with them three days. Each day the tiger's paw was better, and on the third day the cut was quite healed.

So the prince said goodbye to his friends, and the tiger promised help if he was ever in trouble. So the young man rode on. At last he came up with four men who were arguing. Their master had died and had left them all his possessions. There were four things: a bed which would go wherever it was bidden, a bag which could be filled with anything the owner wished, a bowl which was always full of water, and a stick and rope. If the owner of this last said: 'Stick, beat!' it would whack whoever was there and then tie him up with the rope. The trouble was that the men could not decide which of them should have which object. If one said: 'I'll have the bag', the others would all shout: 'No, you won't. I want it.' So the quarrel went on with no end in sight.

The prince said: 'Why waste your strength in quarrelling? Let me decide. I will shoot four arrows into the air. Whoever gets the first arrow shall have the bed. The finder of the second arrow shall have the bag, the third the bowl, and the fourth the stick. How is that for a solution?'

They could think of no better way, so the prince shot his arrows and they went far off into the jungle. Off ran the four men. They were gone a long time, for the trees were dense and the arrows hard to find. The prince sat on the bed, thinking, with the bag, the bowl and the stick beside him. He thought to himself: Perhaps it would be better if these things stayed in my care. If the men have them, they will always be quarrelling. So he said aloud: 'Bed, take me to Princess Labam's country.' Up went the bed into the air, and away it flew over jungle, desert and sea until it came to the land which Princess Labam's father ruled. Then it came down into a field.

The prince said to some men working in the field: 'Whose land is this?'

They said: 'It's Princess Labam's country.' So the prince picked up his treasures and walked along till he

came to a house where an old woman sat. She said: 'Hallo, stranger! Where are you from?'

'A long way off, auntie,' he said. 'Can you put me up for a night?'

'I am sorry, my dear,' she said. 'The king does not allow strangers into his land. If I let you stay here I shall get into trouble.'

'Just one night,' he said. 'It is getting dark, and if I go into the jungle, the wild beasts will surely eat me up. Please let me stay.'

'Very well!' said the old woman. 'But just one night, mind! You must be off in the morning, or we'll both of us be in jail.'

He went into the house, and she began to get dinner ready. 'Wait a minute, auntie!' said the prince, and picked up his bag. He whispered to it: 'Dinner for two, bag', and put in his hand and pulled out two gold plates heaped with good food. So they sat down and ate very well. Afterwards she said; 'I'll just get some water.' 'No need,' said the prince, and picked up his bowl, and sure enough, it was full of clean water.

It was evening, and the room was growing dark. 'Light the lamp, auntie,' said the prince.

'No need!' said the old woman. 'The king allows no light in his kingdom. Every evening the Princess Labam sits on the palace roof, and she is so beautiful she turns night into day. She stays indoors all day. Then at night people can go about their ordinary work and see to finish it.'

When it was quite dark a great light shone from the palace. The princess had got up. She put on her rich robes and jewels, and the light glowed from her. The prince watched her without speaking and glowed too, with happiness. 'How lovely she is!' he thought.

At midnight the princess went indoors and light

faded all over the city. The prince waited until he knew she would be asleep. Then he got up very quietly and sat on the bed. 'Take me to Princess Labam,' he said; and the bed carried him away smoothly and put him down in her room. There lay the princess, fast asleep, and he did not disturb her. He got out his bag and said to it: 'Fetch a large supply of betel-leaf.' It obeyed, and he put the heap of leaves in a corner of the room and went back to the old woman's house.

Next morning the princess's maidservant found the leaves and showed them to the other servants. They each took a handful and began to chew it. The princess noticed and said: 'Where did you get that?'

'We found it by your bed,' they replied, and she was puzzled.

Back at the house the old woman was urging the young man to go home. 'You can't stay here any longer,' she said, 'or I shall be in serious trouble.'

'Oh auntie!' said the prince. 'I don't feel at all well today. Just let me stay till tomorrow.'

'Very well,' said the old woman. So there he was, safe for another day, and they ate well with the help of the bag.

That evening Princess Labam lit up the city as usual, and then went to bed. The prince visited her again, and told the bag to bring him a fine shawl. It gave him a most beautiful shawl, all gold and silver thread, and he spread it over the sleeping princess.

In the morning the princess awoke and was delighted to find what had come during the night. She ran at once to her mother and said: 'Look! Surely the goddess must have visited me.' Her mother was very surprised, but agreed that such a fine gift must have come from God.

At the house the old woman said: 'Now you really must go today.'

'Listen, auntie,' said the prince. 'I've grown so fond of you. I must stay a day or two longer. I'll keep well under cover and no one will know. Please don't throw me out.' And of course she agreed.

The same thing happened that night. The princess lit up the city, and then went to bed. As soon as he dared the prince went to her room. This time he asked the bag for a jewelled ring. When he had it he took Princess Labam very gently by the hand to put it on. She woke up with a start. 'Who's that?' she said nervously. 'What are you doing in my room?'

'Don't be afraid,' he said. 'You are in no danger. I am not a thief. My father is a king. The hiraman told me about you, and so I left my home and my parents to come to see you. Believe me, I love you dearly.'

'Well,' said Princess Labam, 'since you are of royal blood I will not have you arrested and killed. In fact I see that you are a good-looking young man and I believe that you are kind. I shall tell my father that I want to marry you.'

The prince went back in great good humour. In the morning the princess told her father what had happened. 'That is all very well,' said the king. 'But I shall want to know what the young man is capable of.' Then he decreed that the prince must perform a task before he could be accepted as Princess Labam's husband. He must take eighty pounds of mustard seed and crush the oil out of it in a single day. If he failed he must die.

Meanwhile the young prince was telling the old woman that he was going to marry the princess. 'Don't think of it!' she cried. 'You don't know how many princes and kings have wanted her and they are all dead. The king won't let her go. He sets all her suitors impossible tasks and has them put to death. Go home at once and forget all about her.' But he would not listen.

Now the prince made his way to the palace and presented himself as the princess's suitor. He was led into a barn where there was a great pile of mustard seed, and told to set to work crushing it. He sat down on the heap and thought gloomily about his task. There was not a hope that he could complete it in time. 'If only I had a friend to help me,' he said. Then he thought about the ant king, and as he did so the creature appeared. The prince explained his problem. 'Don't you worry!' said the ant. 'Just you take a little rest and leave it all to me.' So the prince lay down and slept, and the ant king called up a multitude of his subjects and they very quickly crushed the seed.

When the prince awoke he was mightily pleased. He called the king, but the king said: 'Very good! Now for the second task. In the palace stables there is a cage and in it there are two demons. I don't know what to do with them, so you had better kill them—if you can. If not, I suppose they will kill you.' He thought to himself: 'This way I can't lose. If the demons win I'll be rid of this young man. If he wins, and it is not likely, at least I'll be rid of the demons.'

The prince went to the stable and peered through the bars of the cage. What ugly demons they were! And how angry after being shut up for so long! 'I shall never win a fight with them,' he said to himself. 'What I need is a big strong friend.' The memory of the tiger came to him, and at once the great beast stood before him. 'What is the trouble?' he growled.

The prince explained his difficulty. 'No trouble!' said the tiger cheerfully. 'My wife and I will be

pleased to take on these two little demons.' So the
tiger called his mate. With a blow of his great paw he
broke the bars of the cage, and out came the demons.
What a fight that was! Both sides bit and struck and
clawed, but in the end the demons lay dead on the
stable floor. The prince praised his friends and tied up
their wounds, then he went off and told the king that
his task was done.

'Well done!' said the king. 'Now there is just a little
task to be done. High up in the sky I keep a
kettledrum. Go up and sound a good rat-a-tat-tat on
it.'

The king thought he had him there, but the new
task bothered the prince not at all. He just sat on his
bed and gave it his orders. The bed shot up into the air
and flew to the drum. The prince beat it heartily and
made a noise like a thunder-storm. Down came the
prince and went to see the king again. Still he would
not give up his daughter to this troublesome young
man.

'Come with me,' he said, and took the prince to a
courtyard where there was a great fallen tree. 'Take
this' he said, and gave the young man an axe with a
blade made of wax. 'By tomorrow morning you must
cut the tree-trunk in two with the axe,' he said.

This last task had him beaten. The prince thought
and thought, and could find no way to do the job.
What is more he had used all his friends, and his
treasures were no use this time. That night he sat on the
bed and went to see Princess Labam. 'I had to see you
once more,' he said. 'Tomorrow your father will have
me killed.' And he told her all about the impossible
task.

'Don't you worry,' said the princess. 'I can help you
with this task.' Then she pulled a single hair out of her

head, and it was long and fine and strong. 'Take this', she said, 'and lay it on the cutting-edge of the axe.'

In the morning the prince went to the courtyard and picked up the axe. He laid the hair along the blade and tied it at each end. Then, very carefully, he raised the axe and touched the tree-trunk with it. At once the great tree fell apart.

The king could think of no more tasks and no more excuses. 'You shall have my daughter,' he said. So they were married, and a happy day that was. Soon afterwards they travelled to the prince's own country, taking with them many gifts and treasures. There they lived happily for many years. The prince's bed and bag and bowl continued to be useful, but as he managed to stay at peace with his neighbours he never needed to use his stick.

The Brave Potter

It was a dreadful night. The rain came lashing down and the thunder crashed. Even the tiger was afraid. He crawled under the shelter of a poor, tumbledown hut where an old woman lived, and lay there flinching every time the lightning flashed.

The old woman was unhappy too. She was worried because the roof leaked and her possessions were getting soaked. She kept dragging furniture from one place to another to avoid the water, but it was coming through everywhere. 'Oh dear, oh dear!' she grumbled to herself. 'What a mess! Surely the roof will come down next. I'm worn out with the wet. If a wild beast, a bear or a tiger, were to come in now, it wouldn't be half as bad as this constant dripping.'

The tiger thought: 'I wonder what that is. Constant dripping must be a fearsome creature if it frightens her more than I would.' When, shortly afterwards, she dropped her big iron cooking-pot and it made a great clanging noise, the tiger said: 'Perhaps that is constant dripping!'

Just then a potter came along the road. Someone had paid him for making a fine pot that day, and the potter had spent the evening drinking to his good fortune. Now he was somewhat the worse for drink. He had lost his donkey and was looking for it as well as his blurred eyes and the wild weather would let him.

The potter lurched up to the hut and saw the tiger lying against the wall. In the dark he mistook the animal for his lost donkey. He grabbed it by the ear, gave it a kick and a thump, and dragged it to its feet.

'Get up, you four-footed devil!' he shouted, 'or I'll break every bone in your body.'

The tiger was thoroughly confused. 'What can this be?' he said to himself. 'Surely this fellow must be the constant dripping the old woman was frightened of. He can hand out some hard blows, and I am sure I'm more afraid of him than I would be of a bear.'

In this confused state the tiger stood quietly while the potter scrambled on his back. Then the drunkard kicked the great beast in the ribs and made him carry him all the way home. There the potter dismounted and tied the tiger securely to the tethering-post. Then he staggered off to bed.

In the morning the potter's wife looked out of the window and got the surprise of her life. There was an enormous tiger tied up to the donkey's post. She shook her husband awake. 'Do you know what is outside?' she screamed.

'Yes, my old donkey,' yawned the potter.

'Look for yourself,' she said. What a strange thing! The potter felt himself all over for wounds, but no! He was unhurt, and there was the savage animal he must have ridden home last night.

As you might guess, the news of what the potter had done soon got around. All the neighbours came along to gaze at the helpless beast. Someone sent a message to the king, telling him about the brave potter, and the whole court turned out to see it for themselves.

Now it happened that the tiger was a very famous one, for it had been terrifying the whole countryside for a long time. Many a goat and ox it had eaten, and a few babies too, and no one was sorry to see it put out of harm's way. When the king was told how his kingdom had been saved, he could not do enough for the potter. Money and land he gave him and a fine house, and he made him commander of a troop of his army.

This was fine for the potter, who accepted every gift and honour as his due. But when, shortly afterwards, a neighbouring king declared war and moved his army to the frontier, everyone from the frightened king himself to the smallest servant in the palace looked to the brave potter to save them from their enemy.

The king sent for the potter and said. 'I am putting you in command of all my forces. Go out and do battle for your king and country.'

'Very well,' said the potter. 'I will do this gladly. One who binds tigers has no fear of men! But before I lead your army, I will go out alone and find out for myself the position and strength of the enemy.'

He went home and told his wife: 'They have made me commander-in-chief. There is just one difficulty. I must ride at the head of the army, and I have never been on a horse in my life, and I am too old to start now. Can you find me a nice quiet little pony?'

Before she could do this, a messenger arrived from the king. His Majesty had sent a gift to his gallant general, a horse. This was an enormous animal and so fierce and lively that it had to be led between two trained elephants. 'That does it!' said the potter. 'I can't ride a pony now or the king will be insulted. But how the devil am I to ride this monster?'

'Don't worry,' said his wife. 'You have only got to mount. Then I will tie you on with a strong rope, and if you start out at night no one will notice.'

'All right,' he said, and that night he came to where the great horse was tethered. 'The saddle is higher than my head,' he grumbled. 'How do I get up there?'

'Jump!' she said, and he did, but came down harder than he went up. He tried several times, but with no better luck.

'Which way should I be facing?' he puffed.

'The horse's head, of course.'

'Oh yes!', and he made a mighty leap and landed in the saddle, but, alas, with his face to the horse's tail. She hauled him down, and he tried again, and again, and again.

At last, bruised all over but still not discouraged, he managed to scramble into the saddle the right way round. 'Quick!' he shouted to his wife. 'Tie me in before I fall.' And she tied his feet to the stirrups, and wound rope around his waist and his neck and tied it to the horse's neck and body and tail.

The horse had been getting more and more puzzled and angry. Now when he felt all those ropes he began to kick and rear and snort, and at last he broke away and galloped off across country.

'Wife!' shouted the potter. 'You forgot to tie my hands.'

'Never mind,' she said. 'Hang on to his mane.'

Away went the horse, and away too went the potter because he had no choice. Hedges and ditches were nothing; the horse just sailed over them, and rivers and plains and mountains went by like a dream—or a nightmare. The potter kept his eyes shut most of the time, but at last he managed to open them and saw in front of him the enemy camp and the army lined up in battle order.

The potter did not like this one bit. Commander-in-chief he might be, but he wasn't going to fight the enemy all on his own, if he could help it. He let go of the horse's mane with one hand and caught hold of a young tree by the trunk, hoping to check his headlong charge. But the horse was going too fast, and the tree just came up by the roots.

The enemy had been warned that they were up

against a fearless soldier who rode on tigers. When they saw what happened, they broke ranks. 'Look!' they shouted. 'Here comes a giant.' And they ran to their general screaming: 'It's all up with us! The enemy commander tears up great trees by the roots and waves them at us. We will fight men but not monsters.' The panic spread through the army, and they all fled for their lives.

The potter rode into an empty camp. He was worn out and so was his horse. Just outside the commander's tent the rope broke and the potter fell off. He picked himself up, and found that he was in possession of a military camp, full of arms and treasure; and in the commander's tent he found a hastily written letter surrendering unconditionally.

The potter took the letter and went home. This time he walked, and his horse followed quietly at his heels. When he got to his house, he told his wife: 'I've had a terrible night. I've ridden all round the world and back again. I'll tell you about it when I've had a sleep. But send this letter to the king at once, and make the messenger ride my horse. The king will see how tired it is and what an adventure I have had. Besides, if the messenger rides it today, I shan't need to ride it tomorrow, for I should surely fall off.'

Next morning the potter walked to the palace. Everyone who saw him said: 'What a hero! And what modesty! He's not the one to go prancing up to the king on his charger. He won the war single-handed, and now he walks to the palace like any humble fellow. Give him a cheer!' And cheering crowds went with him all the way.

After that no enemy ever dared to threaten the kingdom. And the potter, laden with wealth and honours, lived the rest of his life in peace and contentment.

The Ivory City

The prince and his friend the prime minister's son were a carefree couple, filling their days with thoughtless amusement.

One day they were out walking and practising their archery, and the prince fired at a bird on a window-sill. The bird flew up unhurt, and the prince and his friend walked on, laughing at the poor shot.

What they did not know was that the arrow had gone through the window and hit a woman sitting inside. She was a merchant's wife, and when he found her lying, apparently dead, he at once raised the alarm. But she was not dead. The arrow had grazed her breast and she had fainted from the shock. When she came to herself, she told her husband that a young man in the street had shot an arrow at her. The husband was so angry that he went and complained to the king, and the king said that the criminal must be found and punished. He ordered all the young men of the city to walk below the woman's window, so that she could pick out the one who had done this wicked deed.

A big crowd assembled, and among them were the prince and his friend, who had gone along to see the fun. The merchant's wife recognized the prince at once, and the young man was taken before his father.

'I am ashamed,' said the king. 'My own son is a criminal! And my prime minister's son is no better. Off with their heads!'

'Just wait a moment, Your Majesty,' said the prime minister. 'You should not be hasty. Let us question the boys.' And, turning to them, he said: 'Why did you do this dreadful thing?'

'It was an accident,' said the prince. 'I fired at a bird, and missed, and never knew that my arrow had hurt anyone. I would never have done such a thing deliberately.'

The king and his minister talked for a long time, and in the end the king relented. The young men would not be executed, but they must go into exile.

So, next day a sad procession left the palace. The two friends were going into exile, with a company of soldiers to see them on their way. When they reached the border of the kingdom, the soldiers left them and they were on their own. They rode on until they reached a village where they decided to stay the night. The prince made a fire while his friend went into the village to buy food. He was gone a long time and the prince became impatient. He walked down to a small stream and thought that he would find its source. This was not far away, a very beautiful lake covered with lotus flowers. He knelt to drink and, to his surprise, saw a lovely young woman reflected in the water. He looked up quickly but could see no one. Again he drank and again saw the image. This time he looked across to the opposite bank and there was the woman, so delicate and frail that she seemed hardly to belong to this world. The prince looked once and found himself deeply in love. The pain of this was so great that he fell fainting.

Meanwhile his friend had come back to camp with the food. There was the fire and the horses and all their goods, but no prince. He noticed footprints in the soft ground by the stream and followed these to the lake, and there lay the prince.

In a panic he lifted the young man's head and bathed his face with water from the lake. After a minute or two the prince opened his eyes and looked

around wildly. 'Where is she?' he said. 'I must find her.'

'There is no one here,' said his friend. 'Who do you think you saw?'

'I saw the loveliest woman in the world. I saw her only for a moment, for when she knew I had seen her she hid her face in the lotus flowers. But she picked up an ivory box and held it out to me. I must have her for my wife.'

'My dear brother,' said his friend. 'I know who you have seen. It is Gulizar, the fairy princess of the Ivory City. We shall find her, and I will do my best to persuade her to marry you.'

So they continued on their journey, and after many adventures they came at last to a city of pure white palaces, and this was the Ivory City. They found a humble cottage where an old woman agreed to give them lodging while they stayed in the city.

Next morning, the young men noticed that the old woman had dressed in her best and combed her hair carefully. 'You are looking very fine,' said the prince. 'Where are you off to, auntie?'

'I am going to see my daughter,' she said proudly. 'She is a servant of the princess Gulizar and lives in the royal palace.'

'Don't tell her anything about us,' said the prime minister's son. He knew that she was a great gossip, and his warning would only make sure that she told her daughter about the two visitors. This way the news of their arrival would reach the princess.

Sure enough, as soon as she reached the palace the old woman told her daughter about her lodgers, and the daughter ran and told the princess. Her mistress pretended to be angry and gave her a beating, saying that she was never to mention the strangers again.

When she got home, the old woman told her guests what had happened. The prince was distressed, but his friend said: 'Nonsense! She is only pretending. She is really excited to hear about you and is longing to meet you.' And this the prince was very willing to believe.

Princess Gulizar arranged that when the old woman came to the palace next time, a servant was to run in and shout that an elephant had run mad and was threatening to knock down her house. This was done, and, as expected, the old woman fell into a great fright and wanted to get home quickly. The princess let her use a magic swing which would take the swinger wherever she wished. The old woman jumped in, the swing swung high, and the old woman landed in her own garden. But of course no elephant was to be seen.

'This is a good sign,' said the prince's friend. 'The princess is preparing to meet you.'

Two nights later there was no moon, and in the darkness the prince and his friend crept out, sat themselves in the swing, and said: 'To the palace!' And there they were. The princess was standing in the garden, waiting.

'At last, my love!' she said, and the prince took her in his arms. And they plighted their troth before the night was out.

With the help of the magic swing the prince was able to visit the princess every night, and he always took his good friend with him. The princess was not pleased about this; she might be in love with the prince, but the prime minister's son she hated. She made up her mind to get rid of him, so she prepared a tasty meal and mixed strong poison with it. Then she sent the food to the young man with a friendly message of greeting.

He was surprised to see it, because he knew she had no love for him. However, he did not want to offend her, so he took the food outside to eat beside a stream. He put the dish on the grass while he went to wash his hands. When he got back, the grass around the dish had turned a pale yellow. He took out a little of the food and threw it on the ground. A crow flew down and pecked at it and dropped dead.

That evening the prince noticed that his friend was pale and silent. 'What is the matter?'

'You see this dish. It is full of poison. Someone sent it to me today as a special favour, and I nearly ate it.'

'Who did this dreadful thing?' said the prince angrily. 'Tell me his name and I will put him to death.'

'It was the princess Gulizar.'

'I cannot believe it,' said the prince.

'Listen,' said his friend. 'When next you see the princess, pretend to be weeping. She will ask you why, and you must tell her it is because your friend is dead. Then give her a little of this wine to drink. It is very strong and very soon she will fall into a deep sleep. While she is unconscious, take this shovel and heat it in the fire, then you must touch her back with it. Take away her pearl necklace and then leave her. Do what I say, for your happiness depends on it.'

This seemed very strange to the prince, but his friend had always been faithful to him and so he obeyed. He left Gulizar still asleep, and then he and his friend dressed up, the friend as a fakir and the prince as his servant. They rode off and hid in a graveyard on the edge of the city.

When Gulizar awoke she felt a smarting pain in the back. This worried her less than the loss of her necklace which had disappeared. She went at once to

her father, the king, and complained about the theft.
The king was very angry, and he had the crime
proclaimed throughout his kingdom.

'Good!' said the prime minister's son when he
heard. 'This is what we wanted. Now, my prince, take
the necklace and try to sell it in the bazaar.'

The prince took it, but the first goldsmith he went
to recognized it at once and told the police. The prince
explained that he had got the necklace from his
master, the fakir, and so they went and found him in
the graveyard. He was deep in prayer and no one, not
even the king, dared to interrupt until he had finished.

'Tell me, holy one,' said the king. 'Where did you
get this necklace?'

'Last night,' said the mock-fakir, 'we were kneeling
here praying to the gods when a ghoul, in the disguise
of a princess, came to the graveyard, dug up a newly-
buried body, and began to eat it. I was so angry that I
picked my shovel out of the fire and hit her with it and
she ran away. But as she ran she dropped her
necklace.'

'But this cannot be,' said the king. 'The necklace
belongs to my own daughter.'

'Send for her,' said the fakir, 'and examine her back.
If it is burned, then she is the ghoul.'

There was the mark, clear upon her back. The king
flew into a rage and wanted to have her killed out of
hand. But the fakir declared that, as her offence was
against the dead, the punishment should be at his
hands. And he had her shut in a cage and put down in
the graveyard. When night came, the fakir and his
servant threw off their disguises, let the princess out of
her prison and put a soothing ointment on her back.
Then they took her on their horses and rode until
morning.

In the daylight, the prime minister's son showed the princess the dish of poison and said: 'Do you know what this is?' She was ashamed and wept bitterly. He forgave her, and said that from that moment they would be good friends.

Now the prince wanted nothing but to be at peace with his father again. They wrote a letter to the prime minister, telling him everything, and he pleaded with the king. The king insisted that, first of all, his son must tell the whole truth to Gulizar's father. So another letter was sent, this time to this king, and he was not too pleased to have been fooled by a mock-fakir. He was glad however to know that his dearly-loved daughter was alive and well, and he readily agreed to her marriage.

The wedding took place at once, and what a splendid affair it was too! Then the prince and his lovely royal bride, and his dear friend too, set out for home, riding on gaily painted elephants and accompanied by a troop of mounted soldiers. When the king saw them coming, he was happy to forgive his son the folly of his youth, and so too was the unfortunate wounded lady who had been the cause of all the trouble.

Our Brahman is a Poet

In our village there lives a Brahman who is not only poor, he is stupid too. How he manages to survive is a mystery. He begs for a living and as often as not he goes to bed hungry. To make matters a great deal worse he is a married man, and his wife's tongue is sharper than the barber's razor. The poor fellow is afraid to go out in the morning for fear of what he will find in the hard world, and afraid to go home at night because of what his wife has in store for him. What a life!

One morning she started up in her usual way. 'I don't know why I married you. You're fit for nothing. Look at those Brahmans who call at the Raja's house every day. They spin off a line or two of verse, and likely enough they come away with a purse of silver or gold. Their wives don't have to worry about where the next meal is coming from, or whether the children run around naked. Just look at you. You idle around the village and come home with a couple of pice or nothing.'

'What can I do?' said the poor man. 'I don't know how to start making verses, and I don't know a pundit who could teach me. What do you want me to do?'

'I want you out of this house,' said his loving wife, and she picked up her broom and swept him out of the door.

He wandered through the village, quite at a loss how to pass the day. In time he came to a garden and sat down at the foot of a tree to think. Only gloomy thoughts would come to his mind, and not one idea of how to make some money. As he sat there, a pig came blundering into the garden and began to rub her fat body against the tree. The scratching eased her itches and she was enjoying herself.

The Brahman watched the pig for a time without thinking. Then suddenly he jumped into the air and shouted: 'I've got it!' He had no paper, so he plucked a palm leaf and wrote on it:

Rub, rub, rub! Rub with all your might.
What this rubbing's all about is clear as daylight.

Then he rubbed his hands together with great satisfaction, and said to himself: 'There! I am a poet at last. I shall go to the Raja at once and see what reward he will have for my efforts.' And off he went in haste.

When he got to the palace, the Raja had left the
court and all his attendants had gone to their own
rooms. The Brahman waited, hoping that someone
would come and take notice of him. As time went by
he became more and more nervous. 'Suppose the Raja
doesn't like my poem,' he said; 'He'll most likely have
me beaten. I'll not stay to risk that. I will just leave the
poem lying here and see what happens.'

He put the leaf where the Raja would sit next
morning while he was being shaved; then he hurried
home to his wife's loving welcome. 'So you are
keeping me waiting again,' was her greeting.

'Don't nag!' said the Brahman boldly. 'Our fortune
may be made. I wrote a verse for the Raja today and he
will see it tomorrow. Who knows? He may make you
his queen.'

Next morning the Raja got up and went down to be
shaved. There stood the barber sharpening his razor.

Now the queen and the chief of police had plotted
together to kill the Raja, and today was the day. They
had bribed the barber to cut his master's throat while
shaving him. The barber was feeling very nervous,
and he rubbed and rubbed the razor blade, trying to
build up courage to do the deed.

The Raja sat waiting. His eye fell on the palm leaf,
and he picked it up idly and read:

Rub, rub, rub! Rub with all your might.
What this rubbing's all about is clear as daylight.

'What is all this rubbish?' thought the Raja and read
the words out aloud. The barber was horrified. He
threw himself on the ground and embraced the Raja's
feet, shouting: 'Mercy, Lord! I never meant to do it.
The Rani and the Kotwal made me agree. I would
never kill my king.'

'What in the name of all the devils are you talking about?' said the Raja irritably. 'Get up, man, and stop babbling. What is all this about the Rani and the Kotwal?'

The barber said: 'They made me promise to cut your throat today. I didn't want to do it. Thank goodness that you discovered the plot.'

'Well, well!' said the Raja. 'That was quite a good poem I read just now. I must find the author.'

He made enquiries and traced the poem to the Brahman, and then ordered that worthy fellow to come before him. The Brahman was terrified. He was sure that he was to be punished for his bad verse. When the Raja's guards came and took him by the arms, all hope went from him and he wept bitterly as he was led in front of the Raja.

'Did you write this verse, fellow?' asked the Raja.

'Yes, Maharaj,' said the Brahman. 'I meant no harm.'

'You have saved my life,' said the Raja. 'How can I reward you? Half my kingdom would not be too great a reward. But I fancy that you would not find much use for that. How would you like enough money for two good meals a day from today until your life ends?'

And while the Brahman was collecting his first day's pension, the Raja took his guard and went to pay a call on the Rani and the Kotwal.

I told you our Brahman is stupid. If you saw him now, you would say that it is better to be lucky than clever.

Sivalu the Match-Maker

There was a weaver who had come down in the world. The family had once lived in style, but father had squandered his money unwisely and now all that was left of all that wealth was a single squalid hut.

A jackal had his den nearby. The animal had a kind heart, and he was moved by the weaver's wretchedness. Besides, he loved to interfere in other people's lives. So he said to the weaver one day: 'Friend, it pleases me not at all to see you so poor and unhappy. I have a fancy to improve your lot. What would you say to a princess for a wife?'

'That would be a joke,' said the young man, 'and it will happen, I dare say, when the sun rises in the west.'

'We shall see,' said the jackal.

Next morning the jackal was up early. He set out for the king's palace at a brisk trot. On the way he passed a betel plantation and, jumping the fence easily, he helped himself to a good supply of leaves. When he reached the palace he had no trouble at all in slipping past the guards. He settled down by the side of the tank and waited. He knew very well that the princess was in the habit of coming here every morning to take her bath. Sure enough, here she came with her maidens, laughing and playing. When she saw the jackal she stopped laughing. 'Drive the nasty thing away!' she told the ladies, and they came and flapped their scarves at him.

Instead of running away, the jackal stretched himself lazily and gave a great yawn. Then he took a mouthful of betel-leaves and began to chew. The ladies were amazed at such behaviour. 'What's this?' they said. 'Here only wealthy people can afford to chew betel. What kind of beast is a jackal who does it?'

They went and told the princess, and she called the jackal to her. 'Where are you from, Sivalu?' she asked. 'Surely it must be a very wealthy country if jackals chew betel.'

'My dear princess,' said Sivalu. 'You wouldn't believe the wealth of my country. Betel grows like grass. Even cows and dogs chew it. We're not short of anything.'

'What a happy country that must be!' said the princess. 'And is your king equally happy?'

'He is happy enough,' said the jackal. 'In fact he lacks only one thing, and that is a wife. For the rest, his palace is that of the king of heaven compared to your little house. You see, he is the richest man in the world.'

This interested the princess greatly. She ran and told her mother, and the queen decided that she too wanted to talk to the remarkable jackal. Sivalu came to her room, not hurrying himself, and stood before the queen, chewing in a refined fashion.

'Tell me about your king,' said the queen. 'How is it that he has not married?'

'He has never seen a princess worthy of him,' said Sivalu. 'They have come from far and wide to woo him, but he has fine taste and not one of them has pleased him. What a princess that must be who succeeds in pleasing my lord!'

'Tell me, Sivalu,' said the queen. 'What do you think of our princess? Don't you think that she has a rare beauty?'

'She is pretty enough, in an ordinary sort of way.'

'Would you be good enough to consider', said the queen, 'telling your king about her. If you use your words aright, he will surely take a fancy to her and want her for his wife. To tell the truth, it is time she married. She has had plenty of suitors, but none high enough in rank and wealth to deserve her. Now it seems clear that your master would suit her very well, and I should like the match to take place.'

'And what does the king say?' asked the jackal.

'The king always says what I say,' said the queen. 'See, I'll send for him.'

She did, and he came in a great hurry. 'Whatever you think, my dear,' he said when he had heard her proposal, and so the jackal was authorised to make a firm proposition to his master.

'Lord of the loom! You are made!' the jackal told the weaver. 'A great king wants you for his son-in-law, and, what is more, so does a great queen. But you must play it carefully, or we shall both be in serious trouble. Remember that you are a great king yourself, and behave like one.'

Then he told the weaver all that had happened, and the young man readily left it to him to make all the plans.

After a suitable interval the jackal went back to the palace. He strutted in, chewing and spitting and altogether looking like a person of great importance. To the king and queen he said: 'Yes, it looks as if all goes very well. My master is by no means opposed to the match. I had to work hard on him, but in the end I think I may say that my will has prevailed. We have reached the stage when a date may be fixed for the wedding.'

'Splendid!' said the queen, and the king nodded gratefully.

'There is just one thing,' said the jackal. 'My master wants to make a good show at his wedding. He wants to bring a suitable escort of soldiers. Now this may give you a problem. If he brings all the soldiers and horses and elephants he wants, you will be hard pushed to find stabling and food for them all, and I fear that you will be ruined. Now I will try to persuade him to leave most of his forces at the frontier, but I can promise nothing.'

'Do your best, dear Sivalu,' said the queen. 'Otherwise all will be lost.'

Then they studied the omens and decided on the best day for the wedding, and the jackal went home to make his arrangements.

First he gave the bridegroom a long critical look. He was a good-looking young man, but even his best clothes were no more than rags. 'It's no good,' he said. 'You will have to borrow some clothes. Try the washerman. He has usually got a spare suit, and at least it will be clean.'

Then he went off to make his own arrangements. He called first on the jackal king and begged the loan of a thousand wild jackals. Next he visited the king of the crows with a similar request. Lastly he asked the king of the elephants for his help in the same way.

The wedding day came. The weaver put on his borrowed dhoti, and it did not fit him very well. The jackal was joined by the animals promised to him, and they set out on the road. When they were a mile or two from the palace, the jackal called a halt. Then he gave the order, and all the animals cawed and trumpeted and howled according to their kind.

What a row! It sounded as if the sky was splitting. The jackal ran at his best speed to the palace and arrived panting. 'It's no good!' he shouted. 'He would bring them.'

'For heaven's sake!' said the king. 'Take them away. I can't possibly feed that lot. I should have to sell my kingdom and the princess would become a pauper. What good would that do your master? Plead with him to send them home.'

'I'll do my best,' said Sivalu.

He was back shortly. 'All is well,' he said. 'My

master has agreed. He is angry, however, and says that, if you are so mean, he will come without any state whatever. He is coming in plain clothes and on foot. But you had better send a horse for him, or you will be disgraced for ever.'

So the weaver reached the palace on horseback, and, if the crowds were puzzled by his dress, they kept quiet about it. The wedding took place at once, the weaver going through it almost in a dream. Then bride and bridegroom went to bed.

In the night the weaver woke up and could not get to sleep again. He gazed up into the rafters of the state bedroom and said to himself: 'What a place for a loom! Those beams are just right, and there is plenty of space to work.'

The princess was awake too. She thought: 'What kind of a king is this! He seems to know more about weaving than ruling.' In the morning she told her mother what she had heard, and the queen sent for the jackal.

'What a noble man my master is!' said Sivalu. 'He is always thinking of others. You see, weaving is the chief industry of his kingdom, and he never ceases to make improvements in the weaver's lot. Even on his wedding night he was still worrying about them.'

However, the jackal saw that the weaver could not be trusted to keep quiet. He told the king and queen therefore that urgent matters of state made it necessary for his master to go home now. He would travel as he had come, quietly and with just one horse. The princess would ride in a palki.

So they set out and travelled to the outskirts of the weaver's village. Here the jackal sent the palki bearers home, and the princess, in her rich robes and elegant painted feet, had to walk the rest of the way through the mud. They reached the weaver's hut, and the jackal bowed low and said: 'Welcome, Highness, to your palace!'

Well, you may imagine what she thought. But there was nothing she could do about it; besides, she had come to like her quiet, simple husband, and was not unhappy at the thought of sharing her life with him. But poverty she did not care for, and she was determined to improve his fortune.

Being a royal princess, she knew a little useful magic. This is what she did. She bought a bag of flour in the bazaar. She mixed this with water so that it made a smooth paste. Then she took off her clothes and smeared the paste all over her body. It soon dried, and then she rubbed it into little balls. They dropped to the floor and, wonderful though it may seem, turned to gold. She did this several days in succession, and by that time she was as wealthy as she could wish.

Builders and craftsmen were set to work, and they enclosed the little hut with a fine palace. A city was built around the palace, and hundreds of weavers came to live there, working on the finest looms that money could buy. When all was finished, the princess sent a message to her mother and father, inviting them to visit her in her new home. While they were waiting for the royal visitors, Sivalu suggested other improvements to the princess, and so a hospital for sick animals was built, and the city became a favourite place for all kinds of beasts.

At last the king and queen arrived. The streets were covered with silk. Animals lined the road, all of them chewing betel and spitting like humans. As the state procession came down to the palace, Sivalu walked to meet them and, saluting the king and queen as equals, said: 'There! Didn't I tell you?'

A Note for Parents

Whether or not you believe, as some scholars have, that India was the cradle of the world's folk-tales, you will have seen much that is familiar in the foregoing stories. They may wear exotic Eastern dress, but many of the figures under the costume are old friends. What is the resourceful jackal in *Sivalu the Match-Maker* but *Puss-in-Boots*? And the *Brave Potter* is first cousin, if not a closer relative, to Grimm's *Brave Little Tailor*.

The comparisons could be extended indefinitely. Take for example, the story of *The Princes who Turned Night into Day*. The central idea of a princess whose beauty can generate enough power to illuminate a whole city is a peculiarly Indian concept—it occurs too in a Bengali tale *The Triple Thief* which I have not retold for this collection—and I have not met it in other cultures. But all the other elements in this story are familiar: the prohibited area, the animals whose friendship is earned by kindness, the referee who steals the goods on which he has been asked to adjudicate, the illicit night visits to the princess (most familiar in Andersen's *Tinder-Box*) and the bride-tasks. These are themes which recur all over the world.

However familiar the material, the development of the stories is typically Indian. This is not merely a matter of nomenclature—rajas instead of kings, fakirs instead of beggars. The way of thought is as important as the way of life. These are timeless stories. There is no hint—as there is, for example, in Grimm—of recent historical events. Rajas, Brahmans and peasants are alike untouched by the influence of the British, or the Mahrattas, or the Moghuls. Events take place out of the tide of politics; they belong to a civilization ancient almost beyond imagining and to a changeless society.

In making these stories colloquial and accessible to Western children I have inevitably lost some of their Indian quality. My versions may not please Indian-born readers. Perhaps they will help second-generation English-born Indians to retain or recover some part of their cultural heritage. At least they should enable British children to understand something of the centuries of tradition out of which their new neighbours have grown.

My principal aim, at any rate, has been to pump living blood into the stories, blood which has drained out of them in fifty years or more lying entombed in print.

The preservation of Indian stories is the work of no single person, no Grimm or Asbjornsen. We owe them, as much as anything, to the boredom which succeeded the first flush of excitement over the establishment of the British Raj. The Indian Civil Service were the intellectual cream of the country, and some of the administrators at least married girls with intellects to match their own. The dead hand of convention lay across British-Indian society, however, and the clever girls, with their armies of servants and their idle, gossiping neighbours, had nothing over which to exercise their wits. Interference with the lives of the native population was forbidden, but one could perhaps take a discreet interest in their cultural background. This was the genesis of Flora Annie Steel's *Tales of the Punjab*. Mrs Steel—from whose incomparable book I have not drawn directly for my own collection, because it is readily accessible in a recent edition—was a remarkable woman by the standards of any age. Like other great Victorians—Florence Nightingale or Octavia Hill—she had dynamic energy, persistence, and a refusal to mind her own business. She broke through the barrier into Indian culture by having a child. This meant employing an ayah, a children's nurse, who was also necessarily confidante, friend and interpreter. Mrs Steel's ayah, like others of her class, was a repository of old stories which she told to her charges, and the mistress overheard. Mary Frere's *Old Deccan Days* had a similar origin.

Folklore purists might say that this is not direct transmission of the traditional tales. Ayahs were, by virtue of their office, several rungs up the social ladder from the peasants in whose memories the old tales were preserved. This may be strictly true, but tradition is a strong and healthy baby. It may become a little refined in superficial ways but its sturdy limbs remain free of distortion.

A few of the tales which I have retold may have a more lofty social origin. They seem to belong to the class of stories which are told, either by resident or itinerant professional story-tellers, in the courts of kings. They in time came down in the world and were adopted by the people. Most of the tales however are clearly of peasant origin, the oral literature of the cottage and the village square. They betray this origin in their humour, their tough naïvety, their good-humoured satire of the social order. Note how often the Brahman—who is at the top of the caste tree—is portrayed as foolish or ineffectual, but nearly always with some affection and tolerance.

There is a darker side to a society where poverty and disease are endemic, hunger is a daily reality and early death the strongest probability. If some of the stories are frightening, this is because life was frightening for most of the hearers, and a terror told is a terror at least partly exorcised. I hope that our protected children will enjoy meeting these ghosts—mostly comic—and Rakshasis—always horrifying.

My versions, in colloquial modern English, are designed for telling aloud. I have left a few unfamiliar words where these add to the atmosphere of the tales. They are nearly always self-explanatory, but I have added a short glossary and in this I have also tried to explain briefly, caste, the Hindu trinity, and other difficult concepts. I hope that children will not waste time with these, but concentrate their energies on the enjoyment of tales which, whether funny, romantic or tragic, are always full of the love of life.

Glossary

BETEL   a plant; the leaf, spread with areca-nut (sometimes called betel-nut) and lime, is a favourite delicacy

BRAHMAN   see caste

CASTE   the Hindu system of society; the Sanscrit word for caste *varna* means, literally, colour, and the system may date from one imposed by light-skinned conquerors; the four main divisions are: Brahmans, priests; Kshatriyas, warriors; Vaisyas, merchants and farmers; Sudras, labourers; there are many 'outcast' classes below these; the system is hereditary and one cannot rise above or sink below one's caste, nor does it represent one's material standing; in many of the stories the Brahman, who is in the highest class, is very poor and in effect a beggar

DHOTI   a single wrap-around cloth worn by men

FAKIR   holy itinerant beggar

HINDUISM   a very complicated religious system; enough
here to show the Hindu trinity of gods, or of the three
different manifestations of god:

Brahma	Vishnu
the creator	the preserver
married to Saraswati	married to Lakshmi

Shiva
the destroyer
married to Durga
(also known as Bhowani
and Kali)

KOI   the cheapest kind of freshwater fish

KOTWAL   chief of police

KSHATRIYA   see caste

MAHARAJ(AH)   literally great king; overlord of many rajas

MONEY   the currency of the stories is, in order of value:
cowrie, a sea shell used as very small unit of currency;
pice, the smallest coin, four to an anna; anna, the
sixteenth of a rupee; rupee, basic unit with a value of
about 10p; lakh, a hundred thousand rupees, used to
represent a vast sum

PALKI   a palanquin, a mobile bed for ladies of rank or
wealth, carried by a team of bearers

PADDY   rice

PAN   betel, the edible leaf

PIPAL   a large fig tree

PUGRI   head covering worn by men; a turban

PUNDIT   a Brahman specially renowned for learning

RAKSHASI   an ogress, a flesh-eating demon often in the
disguise of a beautiful girl

RAJA(H)   literally king; often in practice little more than a
large landowner

RANI   queen; a raja's wife

SAREE   wrap-around dress worn by all classes of Hindu
women

SINGH   lion

ZEMINDAR   landowner, in effect the leading citizen in a
village